Isabella

(Love without purpose)

Written by

Alaa Zaher

The material and intellectual ownership of this book is subject only to the author, and any modification or copying of the contents of this book without the author's approval will be considered an infringement of the author's intellectual and material rights, as well as the personalities within the book from the author's inspiration, and has no connection to reality and if it is found in reality it is a coincidence. This is a work of fiction. Similarities to real people, places, or events are entirely coincidental.

Copyright © 2024 Alaa Zaher.

Written by Alaa Zaher.

Chapter One

Isabella, a 26-year-old woman, works in a laboratory. She has brown hair and hazel eyes, and she is of average height. While talking on her phone, **Isabella** says:

Isabella: Didn't I tell you, **Amelia**, that I am on my way?

Amelia: Yes, but the manager wants you now. What did you do to make him so angry?

Amelia, a 25-year-old woman, is tall and has blue eyes like the sea.

Isabella: As usual, but the road is extremely congested. I'll be there soon.

Amelia: Okay, **Isabella**, but hurry up.

After half an hour or more, **Isabella** finally arrived at work. **Amelia** met her at the lab's door.

Amelia: All this time, **Isabella**, Mr. **William** is waiting for you in his room. Beware, he is extremely angry.

Isabella went to **William**'s room.

Isabella: May I come in?

William: Yes, come in... Why are you late, **Isabella**?

William, 29 years old, is the son of the lab owner where **Isabella** works. He took over after his father fell ill. He is somewhat tall, with black hair and dark eyes. His skin is olive-toned, and he always shaves his beard because he strongly dislikes letting it grow. **Isabella** stands before **William**.

Isabella: The road was extremely congested.

William: Every day, you come up with a new excuse, **Isabella**. Everyone comes on time except you.

Isabella: I'm really sorry, but today started unusually. I promise to be on time from now on. **Amelia** told me you were very angry with me and that you wanted to see me.

William, with a slight smile: Yes, I told her to tell you that. I know very well that you are always late, so I told her to inform you to hurry up. And here you are now.

Isabella: I truly promise to adhere to work hours from now on.

William: Okay, **Isabella**, go to your work now.

Isabella: Okay.

After leaving **William**'s room, **Isabella** went to work and found **Amelia** in front of her.

Amelia: Who is as lucky as you?

Isabella: What happened, **Amelia**?

Amelia: Nothing. You are the only one here whom **William** can't argue with. I don't know the reason, or maybe I do, but we'll ignore it for now. More importantly, why were you late today? I didn't believe the congested road excuse.

Isabella: I know you won't leave me alone until I tell you.

Amelia: Yes, I'm listening.

Isabella: I dreamed about him again today.

Amelia, slightly annoyed: How long will you keep dreaming about him and waiting for him? It's been five years.

Isabella: No, it's been five years, two months, and two days.

Amelia: You count the days he left you. He won't come back after all this time.

Isabella: Listen, I have lost hope that he will return, but I don't understand why he left me. Why did he go? I've been dreaming for a while that he needs me.

Amelia: He would have returned, but he left and abandoned everything behind, even you. He left you with the curse of memories, leaving thousands of questions in your mind since he left. Enough, **Isabella**, let him go.

Isabella: You won't understand, **Amelia**. I thought you were the only one who would understand because you went through something similar.

Amelia: I understand you perfectly, but **Matthew** returned to me after four months. You know that **Ryan** and **Matthew** traveled, and on the same day **Ryan** decided to separate from you, **Matthew** decided to separate from me. But what happened? **Matthew** returned to me after three months and told you that **Ryan** wouldn't come back no matter what.

Isabella: Okay, **Amelia**, close this damn topic that we talk about every day and argue about.

Amelia: We grew up together. I understand you the most, and I understand him the most. You know well how stubborn he is. He won't change his mind.

Isabella: Didn't **Matthew** tell you anything about him?

Amelia: He told me they talk occasionally, but rarely. I think he's busy with his work or he wanted to distance himself from all of us. He distanced himself from me too, I don't know why.

Isabella: I really don't know why he distanced himself like this. My mind is about to explode from thinking about all the details. I remember the smallest details.

Amelia: Focus on your work instead.

Isabella, angrily: **Amelia**.

Amelia: As you wish.

Isabella: Okay, leave me to work.

After a long day at work, everyone in the lab goes home. **Isabella** drives back to her villa, parks her car, and heads to her room to change clothes and rest a little. But before going to bed, she hears her mother knocking on the door.

Isabella: Who is it?

Isabella's mother (**Sophia**): May I come in?

Isabella: Of course, mom, come in.

Sophia sat beside **Isabella** on the edge of the bed and said: You came and rushed to your room without telling me what happened at work today.

Isabella: Nothing, the same as every day. It's the cursed routine.

Sophia: Okay, I want to talk to you about something.

Isabella: What is it?

Sophia: Do you remember our old apartment?

Isabella: Yes, I remember it a little. But why are you reminding me of it?

Sophia: I will tell you, but...

Isabella: What happened, mom? I'm worried.

Sophia: I know you won't agree, but life, my dear, doesn't stop for anyone's departure.

Isabella: Mom, why are you avoiding the subject? What happened?

Sophia, rubbing her hands: Do you remember **Benjamin**?

Isabella: **Benjamin** who?

Sophia: **Benjamin** used to live in the building in front of ours. He was two years older than you. Do you remember him?

Isabella: Do you mean **Benjamin** who had slightly blonde hair?

Sophia: Yes, that's him.

Isabella: Yes, I remember him. What happened to him?

Sophia: He talked to your brother about you again. He wants to meet you even once. I think it's fair to give him a chance. You can't continue like this.

Isabella, sadly: Mom, I want to sleep a little. You know very well my opinion on this matter.

Sophia: **Isabella**, it's been a long time. I know you loved him, but he left. He broke the engagement and left. He traveled far away and didn't even try once to ask about you as you try to do and know his news. You still ask his sister about him until today.

Isabella, moving from her bed: Mom, enough. I'm really tired of this topic. **Amelia** talks to me about the same thing, and so do you, my brother, and my father. I'm fed up. I don't want him back, and I don't want to get engaged again. I tried my luck once, and I won't repeat it.

Sophia, standing: Do you think we will leave you like this?

Isabella's father (**Quentin**) enters **Isabella**'s room upon hearing their voices.

Quentin: **Sophia**, leave her alone to rest.

Sophia: How can I leave her?

Quentin: Let's leave her alone for a while.

Isabella, crying bitterly, heads to her desk to take a small notebook where she writes down all her feelings, the things she fails to tell anyone.

Isabella, holding her pen, with tears flowing, writes: Everyone fights me so I can forget you. How can I forget all these memories and all the years we spent together? I don't know if forgetting me was that easy for you. I always understood what you wanted to say before you said it, but I still don't understand why you left me. You promised me you wouldn't leave me and you broke your promise. You left me to fight alone my fears that only you knew. Is it time to leave your curse and my heart's ailment? Time didn't make me forget, but it made me harsher until I couldn't recognize myself in the mirror.

At the same moment, our hero **Ryan**, with slightly dark skin, dark brown eyes, black hair, and a black beard that adds to his attractiveness, sits on his usual chair since he traveled. He sits holding a picture of a young man in a navy suit looking at a girl beside him while holding her hand. The girl is wearing a dress.

Her hair flows freely with two strands covering part of her eyes, and she laughs a charming laugh.

He escaped his worries to that moment captured by the camera that day. Whenever the days were hard on him, he escaped to that picture. When he traveled, he also escaped to the picture that captured their engagement party together.

Looking at that picture, he gazed at her features he never forgot and spoke to her as if she was standing in front of him.

Ryan: **Isabella**, what are you doing now? Do you really hate me as **Matthew** always tells me? What should I do, **Isabella**? Life has wronged me once again. I don't know how I will survive this time, but I am truly tired. I am tired of our separation. All I want is to return to you, my home, hold you, and forget everything that has passed. I know you have changed a lot. Do you think I haven't asked about you since I left? Every time I communicate with my family and **Matthew**, I ask about your wellbeing before I ask about theirs. Do you think I could find a girl to take your place? No, my heart swore not to beat for another girl, not to fall for any eyes other than yours that sparkle in the sunlight and make me fall in love with them every time as if it were the first time I saw them.

On the other hand, **Amelia** talks to **Matthew** on the phone.

Amelia: Did **Ryan** talk to you today?

Matthew: No, the last time was yesterday, and his voice was a little different.

Amelia: Different how?

Matthew: I don't know, **Amelia**. He only asks about **Isabella**, and whenever I ask about him, he says he is fine, but his voice doesn't say so.

Amelia: Will he stay there?

Matthew: I really don't know, but I am tired of all this. I want us to be like before and go out together.

Amelia: I wish for that too, but I continue with the lie that **Isabella** no longer loves **Ryan**.

Matthew: What will we gain from this, **Amelia**? We both know she loves him more than before and is waiting for his return.

Amelia: Do you want people to say she has no dignity, that he left her five years ago, and she is waiting for his return?

Matthew: But she still loves him, and he still loves her too.

Amelia: No, he doesn't love her. He only wants her to stay attached to him. He loves her love for him only. The one who loves never leaves, no matter the circumstances.

Matthew: I think you're referring to me too with that.

Amelia: But you returned, **Matthew**. You didn't leave me for five years like he did.

Matthew: But he asked about her every day in all those years. He never got tired of asking about her.

Amelia: **Matthew**, I really want **Isabella** to forget **Ryan**. He will not return, and she has stopped her life for him. I want her to continue her life. Did you know that Benjamin wants to propose to **Isabella**?

Matthew, angrily: What? Have you lost your mind, **Amelia**? If **Ryan** knew about this, he would lose part of his mind. He couldn't believe she no longer loved him.

Amelia: Benjamin has loved **Isabella** since childhood. You know he always insisted on talking to her and taking a step towards her, but **Ryan** always prevented this, causing frequent arguments between them.

Matthew: Yes, I remember that. Do you really want him to propose now just because **Ryan** left the country?

Amelia, angrily: What do you want, **Matthew**? Do you really want her to wait for him, to continue suffering while he is in another country? We don't even know why he left her and traveled.

Matthew, angrily: He left because...

Amelia: Why don't you tell me the truth?

Matthew: Why don't you tell **Isabella** that **Ryan** still asks about her? Why are you trying to convince her that he didn't ask about her? What do you want?

Amelia: If I told her that, she would suffer more and keep waiting for him. We don't know when or if he will return. She is trying to forget him, and she will be able to.

Matthew: I need to hang up now to rest, but I really don't understand you anymore.

Amelia: Me neither... Good night.

Matthew: Good night.

They hung up, and each fell asleep.

At three in the morning, **Matthew**'s phone rings. He answers without seeing who is calling.

Matthew, in a low voice: Hello?

Caller: I know you are sleeping now, but I couldn't wait until tomorrow.

Matthew, trying to wake up: Who is this?

Caller: No, sleep has affected you so much that you didn't recognize your only friend's voice.

Matthew: What? **Ryan**, why are you calling me now? It's three in the morning.

Ryan: I know, but I couldn't wait. I'll be back tomorrow morning.

Matthew: What? You're coming back!

Ryan: Yes, will you wait for me at the airport, or will you abandon me?

Matthew: I'll wait for you. It seems I'm destined to suffer because of you.

Ryan, laughing: We'll see who suffers because of whom when I arrive.

Matthew: When will your plane land?

Ryan: At eleven in the morning. **Matthew**, okay, does your family know about this?

Ryan: I want to surprise them. Don't tell anyone, **Matthew**, not even **Isabella**!

Ryan: See you tomorrow, my friend.

Matthew: Okay, I won't tell her. I'll try to get some more sleep.

Ryan: Goodbye, my friend.

Meanwhile, **Ryan** remembers **Isabella** before he left.

Isabella: Will you leave me?

Ryan: I have no other choice.

Isabella: Why can't you find a solution? What will happen if you stay here?

Ryan: **Isabella**, listen to me. It's over. I met you to tell you that I will travel in three days and to tell you that it's best for both of us to continue our lives without each other.

Isabella: **Ryan**, have you changed, or have you always been like this, and I just didn't see it?

Ryan: You have a long life ahead of you. I'm sure you'll meet someone better for you than me, someone created just for you.

Isabella: Didn't you tell me before that we were created for each other, and now you're telling me I'll meet someone else created for me?

Ryan: Please, **Isabella**, I need to go now. I'm really sorry and hope you won't wait for me.

Ryan, standing, took off his ring with great sadness.

Isabella, holding back her tears: Does this mean I won't be able to see you again?

Isabella, waking up in panic: **Isabella**, to herself: What? Did I dream about that day and that moment again? Won't this damned past leave me alone?

At seven in the morning, **Matthew**'s phone rings again.

Matthew: Was I destined not to sleep tonight?

Amelia: It's seven, **Matthew**. Get up and go to work.

Matthew: What work? I'm not going today. Let me sleep.

Amelia: Why aren't you going?

Matthew: Because **Ryan** is coming today.

Amelia: What? Are you serious, or are you still sleeping?

Matthew, realizing he told her: **Amelia**, you won't tell **Isabella** anything.

Amelia: Will he stay here, or will he leave again?

Matthew, getting out of bed: I really don't know. When I hung up with you last night, I went to sleep and woke up to his call telling me he would arrive today at noon.

Amelia: Okay, I'll leave you to rest.

Matthew: You won't tell **Isabella**, right?

Amelia: Yes, because she doesn't deserve to be torn apart again because of him.

After two hours, **Amelia** enters **Isabella**'s lab room.

Amelia: May I come in?

Isabella: Yes, **Amelia**, come in.

Amelia: I couldn't believe what they said.

Isabella, looking at **Amelia** angrily: **Amelia**.

Amelia: What? This is the first time you've come to work early. What happened?

Isabella: I couldn't sleep well, so I came to work.

Amelia: I'm afraid to ask, did you dream about him today too?

Isabella: Yes, I dreamed about the day he left me and went.

Amelia: Until when?

Isabella: I don't know, **Amelia**, but I am trying to continue my life. I have decided to erase all my memories with him. I am sure he won't return again. That's why I came to work early. When I woke up from that dream, I decided it would be the last time I dream of him.

Amelia: **Isabella**, I want to tell you something.

Isabella: Is it about him? I don't want to hear anything related to him.

Amelia: Have you really decided to erase everything you feel towards him?

Isabella, with her eyes filled with tears: Yes, will you leave me now to continue my work?

Amelia: I know you want to cry now, and you hate to cry in front of others, so I'll leave you.

Amelia went to her office and left **Isabella** crying alone.

Isabella, to herself: You won't cry for him again. I've made a vow to myself.

Her tears increased, and she started hitting her desk with her hands strongly while saying: No, you won't cry. You will surely forget him and give Yahya a chance. You will continue your life as if no one named **Ryan** ever passed through your life.

At exactly eleven thirty at the airport, we find **Matthew** standing to receive his lifelong friend **Ryan**.

Matthew, talking to himself: It's been half an hour since the plane arrived. Why hasn't he arrived?

Ryan, coming from behind him: Have you started talking to yourself in my absence?

Matthew, turning to **Ryan**'s voice: **Ryan**!

Ryan: What? I expected a warmer welcome than this.

Matthew, laughing and hugging him: All these years, my friend, I missed everything.

Ryan, stepping back from **Matthew**: Well, **Matthew**, I'm back now, and everything will return to how it was.

Matthew, smiling: Everything? Everything!

Ryan, smiling too: How is she? Did you tell her I would return today?

Matthew: Didn't you tell me not to tell anyone, my friend?

Ryan: And when do you listen to me?

Matthew: Let's go to your house to surprise your family.

Ryan: Wait, how is she really?

Matthew, trying to avoid the answer: Come on, my car is waiting for us.

Ryan: Why are you avoiding the conversation, **Matthew**? I am talking to you.

Ryan followed **Matthew**, who carried the bags and headed towards his car. Inside **Matthew**'s car:

Matthew: Do you want me to call someone from your family and tell them now, or will you wait until we arrive?

Ryan: Don't tell them now.

Matthew, looking at him: Do you want to tell me now or later?

Ryan: Tell you what?

Matthew: Why did you return now?

Ryan, adjusting himself: I thought you'd be happy for my return.

Matthew: Are you crazy? Of course, I'm very happy, but I don't understand. Also, you're not okay. Did something happen there?

Matthew, looking at the streets through the car window: These streets have changed a lot.

Matthew: I understand, you won't tell me. As for the streets, everything has changed, **Ryan**, not just the streets.

Ryan: **Matthew**, I want to be reassured that **Isabella** is still mine only. Is that true?

Matthew: I don't know, man. As you know, that's a personal matter for her.

Ryan: Yes, you're right, but no matter what happens, she is mine only.

Matthew: I won't lie to you, but since I returned, she met me only once. When I told her you told me you wouldn't return at all and not to wait for you, since that day, **Isabella** doesn't talk to me or meet me as if I was the one who left her.

Ryan, smiling: Now I am sure she is still a child as always.

Matthew: Do you still love her? Do you want to tell me that all these years you didn't meet another girl?

Ryan: I won't lie to you. I tried in every way and indeed met others, but every time I saw them, I saw her in them. It's like a curse that has hit both of us since childhood.

Matthew: **Ryan**, you are very late this time.

Ryan, angrily: Why? Did she meet someone else and love him?

Matthew: We have reached your family's house.

Ryan, even angrier: **Matthew**, don't make me angrier. Did **Isabella** love someone else?

Matthew, parking the car: What do you want? Do you think she will forget that you left her and went away? **Ryan**, you left without telling her anything. You left her alone. The girl was shattered.

Ryan, angrily: Are you really saying this, **Matthew**? You know better than anyone how shattered I was alone abroad and the only person who knows why I left her.

Matthew: Yes, I know everything, my friend, but **Isabella**...

Ryan, fearfully: What? What happened? I didn't believe everything you told me. I didn't believe that **Isabella** hated me and loved someone else.

Matthew: Well, **Ryan**, go now and sit with your family. They must have missed you a lot and will be happy to meet you. Rest, and then we will meet and talk about everything again.

Ryan, opening the car door and putting his other hand on **Matthew**'s shoulder: Thank you for everything, my friend.

Matthew: Are you really thanking your brother?

Ryan, smiling: I'm going down now. And don't tell **Amelia** that I've returned so she won't tell **Isabella**.

Matthew, talking to himself in a low voice: You're late, my friend.

Ryan: What did you say?

Matthew: Nothing. I'll come to help you carry your bags.

Matthew and **Ryan** carried the bags and went upstairs. **Ryan**, looking at his old street and the building where he used to live, said: Everything has changed a lot.

Matthew: Look, I'll knock on the door, and when they open, I'll tell them I want everyone for important news. When they all come, you will appear to them.

Ryan, smiling: Everything has changed except your actions.

Matthew knocked on the door while **Ryan** stood hidden. **Ryan**'s sister **Hana**, who is short, with some of **Ryan**'s features, black hair, olive skin, and dark brown eyes, and is 22 years old, opened the door.

Hana: **Matthew**, how are you?

Matthew: Fine. Where is everyone?

Hana, fearfully: Why? Did something happen to **Ryan**?

Matthew: No, don't worry. I just want to tell you something.

Hana: Just a minute, I'll tell dad and mom.

Matthew: Okay.

Hana went to tell them. After three minutes, she returned with her father **Patrick** and mother **Eleanor**.

Hana's father **Patrick**: How are you, **Matthew**? Are you still standing outside? Come in.

Ryan appeared to them, and everyone looked in shock. Tears fell from **Eleanor**'s and **Hana**'s eyes as they hugged him tightly, not believing that this separation finally ended and they were reunited after five years.

Hana, crying in **Ryan**'s arms: **Ryan**, did you return? I can't believe it.

Ryan, trying not to cry too: Yes, I returned.

Ryan, looking at his father: What? Didn't you miss me?

Hana and **Eleanor** stepped back a bit from **Ryan**, and **Patrick** approached **Ryan** and raised his hand to hit him. The slap was so loud that everyone in the street below could hear it. **Ryan** looked at him with great astonishment, his cheek reddened.

Patrick, with tears in his eyes, hugged **Ryan**: I missed you so much.

Ryan, also crying: Then why did you hit me, dad?

Patrick: Do you think you've outgrown me, **Ryan**?

Ryan, stepping back from his father and looking at everyone: I missed you all.

Eleanor: Okay, let's go inside and continue our conversation there. Please come in, **Matthew**. Where did he go?

Ryan, laughing: He left; he still hates these moments.

Everyone went inside.

Hana: Come on, tell us everything that happened to you there.

Ryan: Not now. I want to rest a bit. But where is **Diana**?

Everyone looked at each other in silence.

Ryan: Where is **Diana**? During my travel, whenever I asked you about her, you told me she was fine and stayed silent. In the last three months, she didn't talk to me even once. Where is she?

Chapter Two

Ryan: Where is **Diana**? During my travel, whenever I asked you about her, you told me she was fine and stayed silent. In the last three months, she didn't talk to me even once. Where is she?

After a brief silence,

Ryan, standing: Where is **Diana**? Why are you silent?

Patrick: **Diana** has left.

Ryan: Where to?

Patrick: This is a long story. Rest now, and we will talk about it later.

Ryan, angrily: How? Where is my sister?

Eleanor: Calm down, **Ryan**. **Diana** is fine, but she left the country.

Ryan: When and why didn't you tell me?

Hana: **Ryan**, at that time, we didn't want to disturb you while you were alone. We didn't know your actual situation. You only told us you were fine.

Ryan: That is not a valid reason not to tell me she left.

Ryan, sighing: Okay, tell me where she went.

Patrick: Three months ago, **Diana** received a scholarship, so she went to England.

Ryan: England!!!

Ryan, looking at **Eleanor**: Is this the truth, mom?

Patrick: Are you saying I'm lying?

Ryan: No, I didn't say that, but something inside me says it's not the truth.

Eleanor: No, it is the truth. **Diana** went to England three months ago.

In the lab where **Isabella** and **Amelia** work, specifically in **Isabella**'s office,

Isabella: What happened, **Amelia**? I noticed you have been looking at me for almost an hour.

Amelia didn't answer.

Isabella, holding **Amelia**'s hand: **Amelia**, I'm talking to you.

Amelia: What?

Isabella: Why are you looking at me like that?

Amelia: I want to ask you a question, but you have to tell me the truth.

Isabella: Okay, go ahead.

Amelia: Will you be happy if he returns?

Isabella: Did **Matthew** tell you he is coming back?

Amelia: **Isabella**, I want an answer, not another question.

Isabella: I told you yesterday that I am trying to forget him. Why are you asking such a question now?

Amelia: Nothing, it was just a passing question.

Isabella: Will he come back?

Amelia: I don't know, **Matthew** didn't tell me anything.

Isabella: Okay.

William knocks on the door.

Isabella: Come in.

William, standing: I think work is over, so you both are sitting and talking.

Amelia: What happened, **William**? We only talked for two minutes.

William: Two minutes only!

Amelia: Okay, I'll go back to work and leave you two alone.

Amelia winked at **William**, knowing he wanted to talk to **Isabella** alone.

After **Amelia** left the room,

Isabella: I'm listening to you.

William, smiling: Did I make it that obvious?

Isabella, also smiling: Because if you wanted to tell me something work-related, you would have said it in front of her.

William: But the matter I want to tell you; I think it's right to discuss it outside the lab.

Isabella: Why?

William: You'll know then. Are you doing anything after work?

Isabella: I don't think so.

William: Then we will meet after work.

Isabella: **William**, wait.

William, moving towards the door: I don't listen to excuses.

Isabella: But...

Isabella, talking to herself: He left. What will I do now?

After the workday ended, **Isabella** was standing, talking to **Amelia** in front of the lab.

Isabella: **William** asked me to meet after work.

Amelia: Will you go with him?

Isabella: I don't know. I am very hesitant, but I think it's time to prove to myself that I have erased him from my heart.

Amelia: In my opinion, you should go and listen to him, then sit alone and decide what you want.

Isabella: I will do that.

William approached **Isabella**.

William: I'll wait for you by my car. Don't be late.

Isabella: Wait, I'll come with you now. Goodbye, **Amelia**, see you tomorrow.

Amelia: No, we'll talk when you return, so you can tell me what happened.

Isabella, smiling: How curious you are, **Amelia**.

Amelia, smiling: I guess I'm very curious. Go now, don't make him wait too long.

After **Isabella** followed **William**, **Amelia** noticed her phone ringing.

Amelia, moving: Hello.

Matthew: How are you?

Amelia: I'm fine, and you?

Matthew: I'm fine. We haven't talked since the morning. Tell me, what did you do today?

Amelia, walking: Nothing much, just the usual. I didn't call you; I thought you would be with **Ryan** all day.

Matthew: No, all I did was take him to his family's house and left them together, then I returned home.

Amelia: Are you going out tonight?

Matthew: I haven't talked to him. But he asked me about **Isabella** and whether she still loves him or not.

Amelia: And what did you say to him?

Matthew: I told him everything had changed, but he got very angry. I couldn't tell him that **Benjamin** proposed to her. She told me yesterday that she decided to start a new chapter in her life.

Amelia: **Isabella** went with **William**.

Matthew: Why? Are they going to discuss work outside?

Amelia: I don't think so. I think he will confess something to her.

Matthew: Confess what?!

Amelia: Since **Isabella** and I started working in the lab, I felt that **William** always preferred **Isabella** over everyone else.

Matthew: Strange.

Amelia: What is?

Matthew: At the time **Ryan** returned, **Benjamin** wanted to propose to her, and now you are telling me that **William** will confess something to her.

Amelia: That's life, **Matthew**. Everything goes against what you want. **Isabella** waited for him for five years without getting tired. But now I see her trying to truly remove him from her heart.

Matthew: Why did all this happen? Just five years ago, we were very happy, the four of us. We grew up together, remember?

Everyone envied our connection, the four of us. They always said we would separate because life distracts us from those we love and tests us with those we sacrifice for. But each time, we got closer and closer until they realized we would never part. But now what they told us has happened.

Amelia: I'm tired of this situation too. But who put us in it? Isn't it **Ryan** himself? He broke the vow and left us all behind.

Matthew: **Amelia**, you really don't know anything. Don't judge him without knowing the whole truth. **Isabella** is also at fault.

Amelia: At fault for what? Did she tell him to go?

Matthew: No, but she distanced herself from me for no reason. She hasn't met me since I told her he said he wouldn't return and didn't want her to wait for him.

Amelia: What is the point of that? I don't understand. Why do you want to meet **Isabella** and talk to her?

Matthew: What do you mean, **Amelia**? Since I was born, I've seen **Isabella** as my sister **Ruby**.

Amelia: **Matthew**, I've reached my house now. I'll hang up to rest a bit, and we'll continue our conversation tomorrow.

Matthew: Wait, **Amelia**. What did you really think?

Amelia hung up the phone in **Matthew**'s face.

On the other side, in a fancy café, we find **Isabella** and **William** sitting together.

William: What will you order?

Isabella: Nothing.

William, looking at the waiter: A strong coffee, please.

Waiter: Of course, sir.

Isabella: How did you know?

William: I see you drinking a strong coffee every day before work.

Isabella: And you drink regular coffee, not strong.

William, smiling: Yes, but do you know why?

Isabella: No, tell me.

William: Since childhood, I've liked everything to be just right. I don't like things to be too little or too much, even feelings.

Isabella: How can feelings be just right?

William: Look, **Isabella**. Humans naturally gravitate towards those who give them special attention.

Isabella: Yes, but...

William: I'll explain if you let me.

Isabella: Yes, go ahead. I'm listening.

William: Humans naturally gravitate towards those who give them special attention, but if it exceeds its limits, it turns against them. If it falls short, they avoid it. Let me give you an example. If you see someone neglecting their feelings and not expressing them, you will naturally hate them over time and avoid them. If you see someone who always gives you extra attention, over time, you'll think it's natural and not special. Apply this to everything in life: work, love, everything. That's why I like coffee to be just right. Do you understand now?

Isabella: Yes, I understand, but in my opinion, the opposite is true. The more you care for someone, the more they will naturally love and care for you.

William: They will see then that the world revolves around them only, and your attention will seem natural. If you try to reduce your attention, they will think you denied them something they deserve.

Isabella: But sometimes, when something increases, it becomes better than being just right.

William: Well, we'll see.

Isabella: How?

William, smiling: I'll change the order now. I'll get you a regular coffee, and I'll have a strong coffee, so we both taste what the other experiences.

Isabella: Do you mean to see things from each other's perspective?

William: Yes.

Isabella: Okay, agreed.

William, looking at the waiter: Excuse me.

Waiter: Yes, sir?

William: I'd like to change my order from two strong coffees to one strong and one regular.

Waiter: Okay, sir. Anything else?

William: No, thank you.

Isabella: So why did you initially order two strong coffees?

William: I wanted to see things from your perspective only. Will we talk all night about coffee, or should I tell you what I want to tell you?

Isabella: Yes, tell me, go ahead.

William: Since you graduated and started working in the lab with **Amelia**, do you remember your first day?

Isabella: Yes, I remember, but why?

William: At that time, my father wasn't ill, and he was the one running the lab. But I was also helping him. On your first day, you didn't know I was the owner's son.

Isabella, smiling: Yes, I remember well when we argued. I didn't find anyone more stubborn than me, but then I found you.

William: Yes, and I didn't find anyone who gets angry as easily as you.

Isabella: Okay, but why did you suddenly remember that day?

William: I never forgot it to remember it. Something inside me at that time told me we would get along well, and it happened when my father got ill, and I took over the lab.

Isabella: Can I tell you something?

William: Of course.

Isabella, laughing, showing her beautiful laugh: On the day I was late for work, and **Amelia** told me on the phone that you were very angry and wanted me to get to the lab as soon as possible...

Isabella: When I arrived, I didn't find you angry or anything. You told me I was very lucky because I was the only one who did all this.

William, looking at her charming laugh: But I am the one who is lucky because I see the beauty of your laugh now.

Isabella, realizing and starting to fade her laugh little by little: What?

William, realizing what he said: I mean, I won't allow that again. The coffee has arrived; let's see who the winner is.

Waiter: Anything else, sir?

William: No, thank you.

Isabella: Now I will see how you judge things from your perspective.

William: And me too.

Isabella then took the first sip of coffee.

William: At first, you'll find it lacking something, but if you take another sip, you'll love it and find it really delicious.

Isabella: I see you haven't tasted your coffee yet.

William: I'll taste it, of course.

Isabella took another sip, then another.

William, smiling: Well, it's my turn now.

William took a sip of the cup and found it really strong, not accustomed to it. He took another sip and then put the cup down, unlike **Isabella**, who drank the entire cup.

Isabella: I see you didn't like the strong coffee.

William: No, it's beautiful, but it's really strong. I feel like something is too much in it.

Isabella, smiling: Is the sugar too much, maybe?

William: Yes, but it's not suitable for everything because, as I told you, when something increases, it turns against itself. What did you find?

Isabella: In the first sip, I thought it lacked something, but then I found it delicious, really delicious to have everything just right.

William, laughing: Does this mean you are convinced by my perspective?

Isabella: And you are not convinced by my perspective.

William: A little. If you're finished, I'll ask for the check so I can take you home before it gets too late.

Isabella: **William**, I really don't understand why we came here. Did we really come to decide which coffee is tastier?

William: Think again about everything I told you, and you'll understand what I mean, **Isabella**.

Isabella: Why don't you tell me the truth?

William: Come on, **Isabella**.

Then he turned to the waiter: Excuse me, I want the check.

Isabella got up and went to wait for him outside, finding the weather raining heavily as if the sky wanted to reveal everything inside it. She stood looking at the rain falling on her.

William: Why are you standing like that? You should have waited for me inside the car.

Isabella: I love walking in the rain.

William: I can't fulfill that wish for you now.

Isabella: Why, do you hate the rain?

William: Did you forget, **Isabella**? It's January, and it's very cold now, and the weather is rainy. Let's go to the car.

They got into the car.

William, driving: What are you thinking about?

Isabella: Do you feel the sky is like us?

William: How?

Isabella: I feel like it keeps hiding what's inside and suppressing all its feelings, then suddenly decides to reveal everything inside it as rain.

William: Do you want to do that too?

Isabella: I no longer know what I really want, as if there's a war inside me, and all parties refuse a peace treaty.

William: Maybe you're the one who refuses that treaty.

Isabella: How? Does a person like to remain confused inside like this?

William: Yes, when we find that the truth won't be as we like.

Isabella: Why doesn't everything go as we want?

William: Because it's life, **Isabella**. It won't give us everything.

Isabella, holding back her tears: But it takes everything we love from us.

William: Yes, sometimes because not everything we love is meant for us or is best for us. Always remember that all paths will be paved for you to get only what's meant for you.

Isabella: Okay, why do we love something that's not meant for us?

William: We love it to learn not to love something that's not meant for us. We love it to learn lessons we would have ignored if not for what happened.

Isabella, with tears in her eyes: Imagine wanting something so simple that you cry because it's not yours. You cry because, despite its simplicity, it didn't come true. I didn't even decide anything; I found that others decided for me that I should do. As if I'm running and running, then suddenly falling. Every time I fall, I see a deeper wound that never heals or ends, as if I'm the one who tried and suffered, and others achieved.

William: Maybe you should learn not to run or cling too much.

Isabella, raising her voice: Okay, but how? How not to cling?

William, stopping the car: **Isabella**, that's what I wanted to tell you, to keep everything just right, not less or more than it should be. You tasted the coffee when it was just right and liked it. I meant that not just about coffee. Do you understand now?

William, handing her a tissue: I don't think there's anything worth crying for.

Isabella took the tissue from him.

Isabella: I want to go home now.

William: Okay.

After half an hour, they arrived at the villa where **Isabella** lives.

William: Don't come to work tomorrow. Rest and remember everything I told you.

Isabella: Okay. Thank you for everything.

William: I think the sky told us everything inside, so it stopped raining, just like you.

Isabella, with a faint smile: Goodbye.

William: Goodbye.

The next day at seven in the morning at Isabella's villa:

Sophia: **Isabella**, wake up.

Isabella: I won't go to work today, mom. I want to sleep.

Sophia: Why?

Isabella: Not now, mom.

Sophia: Okay, **Isabella**. When you wake up, we'll talk.

After half an hour, **Isabella**'s phone rings.

Isabella, in a quiet voice, half asleep: Hello.

Amelia: Are you still sleeping?

Isabella: I won't come today, **Amelia**.

Amelia: Why? What happened yesterday, and why didn't you talk to me after you returned?

Isabella: I want to sleep, **Amelia**. I'll tell you later. Goodbye.

Amelia: **Isabella**. Hello?

Amelia, to herself after **Isabella** hung up: What happened? I don't understand.

An hour later, **Amelia** prepared to go to work and found **Matthew** standing in front of her house. She approached him.

Amelia: **Matthew**.

Matthew: Good morning. I wanted to see you and take you to work so we could talk.

Amelia: Good morning. I don't want to talk about this topic, **Matthew**. Every time we talk about **Isabella** and **Ryan**, we end up arguing.

Matthew: Okay, **Amelia**, but all I want to tell you is that **Isabella** is like my sister **Ruby**. I don't know why you were angry yesterday.

Amelia: **Matthew**, I know very well that you treat **Ryan** almost like your brother. We grew up, the four of us, together, but...

Matthew: But what, **Amelia**? I love you. And as I said, **Ryan** is my brother. I would never betray him. I know very well how much he loves **Isabella**, even when he left her.

Amelia: Do you really love me, **Matthew**, or are you just trying to prove something to yourself?

Matthew: Something like what?

Amelia: **Matthew**, I am the person who understands you best.

Matthew, angrily: What do you mean?

Amelia: I want to go to work.

Matthew: Tell me first, what do you mean, **Amelia**?

Amelia: **Matthew**, I think **Ryan**'s return wasn't good for you. It's time you return to your treatment, **Matthew**.

Matthew: Are you mocking me, **Amelia**?

Amelia: No, I'm not mocking you. I'm just telling you the truth and trying to save you before you make a mistake.

Matthew: I already made a mistake when I thought you wouldn't hold my past against me. I made a mistake when I thought I could tell you everything without hesitation and without lying. But now you're throwing the truth I fought to forget in my face.

Amelia: **Matthew**, I'm sorry. **Matthew**, wait.

Matthew left her and walked away, crying.

Chapter Three

After the workday ended, the doorbell of **Isabella**'s villa rang.

Sophia, opening the door: How are you, **Amelia**?

Amelia: Fine, aunt, and you?

Sophia: Fine. Do you know what happened to **Isabella** yesterday?

Amelia: No, what happened?

Sophia: I don't know. Since she returned yesterday, she's been sitting alone in her room and hasn't spoken or eaten anything. This morning, she told me she wouldn't go to work today.

At that moment, **Gabriel**, **Isabella**'s brother, arrived. He is tall and resembles **Isabella** in some features, with brown hair and slightly hazel eyes. He is 24 years old. He approached **Amelia** and **Sophia** and spoke to **Amelia**.

Gabriel: How are you, **Amelia**?

Amelia: Fine. I haven't seen you in a long time.

Sophia: Are you still outside? Please come in, **Amelia**.

Amelia took off the jacket she was wearing and held it in her hand.

Gabriel: Does this mean you really care about my news?

Amelia, smiling: Do you doubt that?

Gabriel: No, not at all, but there's a lot of work, so we didn't meet much.

Amelia: Okay, I'll go in now to see **Isabella**. See you later.

Gabriel: **Amelia**, wait.

Amelia: What?

Gabriel looked at his mother.

Sophia: I'll go to the kitchen.

After **Sophia** left,

Gabriel: I want to ask you for something.

Amelia: What?

Gabriel: We grew up together, and you know that I loved **Ryan** and **Matthew** like my brothers. But...

Amelia: But after **Ryan** left, you didn't love him anymore and distanced yourself from **Matthew** too. Is that what you're going to tell me?

Gabriel: **Amelia**, he won't come back. He left her, and she still refuses anyone who tries to get close to her. I know she told you that **Yahya** wants to propose to her. We all know that **Yahya** is the most deserving person of **Isabella** because he endured everything for her and waited all this time.

Amelia: He came back.

Gabriel: Who?

Amelia: **Ryan**. He returned yesterday.

Gabriel: What? Impossible. Why did he come back now?

Amelia: I don't know.

Gabriel: Does she know?

Amelia: No, I didn't tell her.

Gabriel: **Amelia**, I...

Amelia: **Gabriel**, I know you're worried about **Isabella**, but this time is very different. Do you mind if I see her now?

Gabriel: But...

Amelia walked towards the villa's staircase to go up to **Isabella**'s room.

Amelia: Goodbye, **Gabriel**.

Isabella, opening her room door and seeing **Amelia** laughing while **Gabriel** is angry with her.

Isabella: **Amelia**! When did you come?

Amelia, looking at her: A little while ago, but **Gabriel** was talking to me.

Gabriel: Okay, I'll leave you two to talk now.

He looked at **Amelia** and said: But we'll meet again, and I won't leave you alone.

Amelia, laughing: Okay.

She looked at **Isabella** and found her sad. They both entered the room.

Amelia: What happened yesterday, **Isabella**?

Isabella: I'll tell you everything.

Isabella told her everything that happened yesterday and everything **William** said to her.

Isabella: That's all that happened.

Amelia: Okay, I understand, but I don't understand why you're sad now.

Isabella: I'm trying to find a way out, but I don't know how.

Amelia: A way out of what, **Isabella**?

Isabella: Did you understand what he meant by his words?

Amelia: Did you understand what he meant?

Isabella: Yes, I understood, and that's the main problem.

Amelia: What is it?

Isabella: My excessive love for **Ryan**, my overwhelming emotions for him, my hope that he would return to me after everything that happened. I thought a lot about what **William** said to me. He was right—when everything is just right, it will be better.

Amelia: So, what is your final decision?

Isabella: Do you feel like he wants to tell me something else?

Amelia, smiling: But he won't say it because he told you that when everything is moderate, it will be better, even emotions.

Isabella: Has the time really come?

Amelia's expression turned sad, and she stood looking out of **Isabella**'s window.

Amelia: I think the time has really come for everything to be moderate and for everyone to return to their natural size. Do you know he was right in his words? Maybe the main problem lies in our excessive emotions.

Isabella, looking at her with surprise: What happened? Did you argue with **Matthew** again?

Amelia: Yes.

Isabella, standing next to her and putting her hand on **Amelia**'s shoulder: But why? **Matthew** is completely different from **Ryan**. **Matthew** came back for you.

Amelia: Did he come back for me, really? Does he love me?

Isabella: What do you mean? Since our childhood, you and **Matthew** have loved each other.

Amelia, with tears falling: No, **Isabella**, that's not the truth. You don't know anything.

Isabella: I don't know what?

Amelia: I can't tell you, but I love him so much. Since I was born, I've seen myself only with him.

Isabella: So where is the problem?

Amelia, raising her voice gradually: The problem is with him, not me. The problem is with him. Since childhood, **Isabella**, he hasn't recovered. He hasn't recovered, **Isabella**.

Isabella: Recovered from what?

Amelia: I hurt him a lot today. I told him the truth to his face. He looked at me in a way I'll never forget, as if I shot him with a fiery bullet. He looked at me as if saying, you betrayed me.

Isabella: **Amelia**, I don't understand anything. Recovered from what? Is **Matthew** sick with something?

Amelia, as if in another world, not noticing **Isabella**'s words: He will hate me because of today. He won't come back to me again.

Isabella: **Amelia**, why don't you tell me the whole thing?

Amelia, snapping out of her reverie: No, I can't tell you. I have to go.

Isabella: **Amelia**, wait.

Amelia left, crying. The next day, it was as if nothing happened. **Isabella** and **Amelia** went to work, and **Amelia** still refused to tell **Isabella** the truth about **Matthew**.

At exactly 10:30 AM, **Ryan** was driving his father's car, talking on the phone.

Ryan: How are you today, my friend?

Matthew: I'm fine, and you, my friend?

Ryan: I'm fine, but your voice doesn't seem like you're really fine.

Matthew: No, no, I'm fine.

Ryan: Then where are you?

Matthew: At home. Why?

Ryan: Why didn't you go to work, and you didn't go yesterday either?

Matthew: I'm not feeling well, so I decided not to go today and yesterday.

Ryan: I knew it. I know your voice well. So, we'll do the following: give me the address of **Isabella**'s workplace, and then I'll come to your house to see you.

Matthew: What will you do? Will you tell her the truth?

Ryan: I don't know, but today I woke up to her voice saying my name.

Matthew, laughing: Woke up to what?

Ryan: Don't mock me. That's what really happened. The time has come for everything to return to its place, my friend.

Matthew: I don't think it's a good idea.

Ryan: Give me the address, and I'll see for myself.

Matthew: **Ryan**, she doesn't know you're back.

Ryan: Good, then I'll see her reaction... Come on, give me the address.

Matthew: Okay, I'm not in the mood to argue with you now. The address is...

Matthew gave him the address.

Ryan: Alright, I'll go to her now, then I'll come to you. Do you want me to tell **Amelia** anything?

Matthew: Goodbye, **Ryan**. I'm hanging up.

After an hour, **Ryan** went to the lab and asked about **Isabella**'s office. Someone working there helped him and described the way to her office. He reached the door and knocked.

Isabella: Come in.

Ryan entered with a bouquet of her favorite flowers, finding her as he left her, not much changed. He found his breath accelerating and remembered their engagement day and the picture that brought them together, which helped him overcome every difficulty he faced alone abroad. He remembered how happy everyone was that day, then recalled the day he told her he was leaving and not to wait for him, the most painful day of his life. All of this flashed before his eyes, remembering his voice inside saying:

"Has the time come for us to be together without anything separating us? I know danger still chases me. I know I came back again, fleeing, not out of love. Did you really think I pulled you out of me? How can I forget my little one, my princess, my special girl? We are cursed with love, **Isabella**. How will either of us heal from this?"

All this time, **Isabella** didn't notice him, still looking at the papers in front of her while someone in front of her explained everything that happened in the two days she didn't go to work. **Ryan** snapped out of his reverie and finally spoke.

Ryan: May I come in?

Her pen fell, and she looked at the paper in front of her, her heart racing.

In her thoughts: "Is it really his voice, or am I imagining it? Oh my God, did he come back after all this time? No, I'm not imagining it. This is really his voice, but how?"

The person who was explaining the work details to her fell silent, and **Isabella** looked at **Ryan** in great shock, finding him really there, standing in front of her with her favorite bouquet of flowers. Tears she didn't know where they came from started falling. They looked at each other in intense silence, which was broken by:

Person: Miss **Isabella**, are you okay?

Isabella didn't respond, so the person repeated the question.

Person: Miss **Isabella**, are you okay?

Isabella, tears falling: How did you come back, when, and why?

Ryan to the person: Could you give us a moment, please?

Person, looking at **Isabella**: Should I really leave or wait?

Ryan: She won't listen to you now. Please, leave us alone.

The person left the room, leaving them alone. All this time, **Isabella** kept looking at **Ryan** and crying.

Isabella, with a broken voice: How did you come back?

Ryan: **Isabella**, calm down. I'll tell you everything, but please don't cry. I can't bear your tears.

Isabella, raising her voice: Bear whose tears? Why did you come back, **Ryan**? And what's that in your hand? Flowers? Do you think I'll forgive you just like that?

Ryan: Lower your voice a bit and calm down. We're at your workplace now.

Isabella, raising her voice even more: Do you really care about anything related to me?

Ryan: I'll wait for you at the café next to the lab so we can talk about everything.

Isabella: I don't want you. I'm tired of everything.

Ryan: Fine, listen to me first, then decide what you want.

Amelia, **William**, and everyone working in the lab stood looking at them.

William: Who is this, **Isabella**? And why are you crying like this?

Ryan, looking at him angrily: I'm **Ryan**, and **Isabella** is my fiancée.

Isabella: Whose fiancée? Have you lost your memory? You left me and went away.

Amelia: Why did you come here?

Isabella: Did you know he came back and didn't tell me?

William: I don't understand anything. **Isabella**, can you calm down a bit?

Then he looked at everyone working in the lab and said: Please, everyone, go back to work.

Ryan: I'll wait for you at the café to talk.

Isabella: I won't come.

Ryan, smiling at her: I'll wait for you, **Isabella**.

Ryan left, and **Amelia** and **William** kept looking at her.

William: Is that him?

Amelia: **William**, please leave us alone.

William: Fine. **Isabella**, can you dry your tears?

Isabella sat on her chair, trying to calm down and dry her tears. **William** left.

Isabella: Why didn't you tell me he came back?

Amelia: Will you go and listen to him?

Isabella, angrily: **Amelia**, why didn't you tell me?

Amelia: Because you told me you didn't want to know anything about him again, so I didn't tell you. I feared this would happen, and it did.

Isabella, standing: I'll go and tell him I no longer want him, that I hate him very much, and don't want to see him.

Holding the bouquet of flowers, she continued.

Isabella: And I'll throw this bouquet in his face. I don't want anything from him.

Amelia: **Isabella**, wait, what are you going to do?

Isabella went to him.

In the café near the lab, **Isabella** entered and saw **Ryan** sitting at a table with sunlight reflecting from all directions. He looked at her and smiled.

Ryan: I knew you would come.

Isabella threw the bouquet in his face and said, standing.

Isabella: Why did you come back now?

Ryan, looking into her hazel eyes that became more beautiful in the sunlight: I never left, **Isabella**. I haven't forgotten anything about you. Do you think leaving you was easy? My heart ached every night.

Isabella, loudly enough for everyone in the place to hear: Then why did you travel? Why did you leave me? Do you know what I went through in your absence? No, you don't. I was shattered, I died a thousand times in your absence. Did you come back now after I got over you?

Ryan, looking at her after hearing the last two words, not believing her: Did you get over me? Did you really forget everything?

Isabella, holding back her tears: Yes, I forgot you. There's no one named **Ryan** in my heart anymore. I think you should save your effort because you'll waste it in vain.

Isabella, moving away, a small tear fell from her eye, indicating she was lying and hadn't forgotten him. How could she forget her first love, the first person her heart beat for? He was her childhood, teenage love, and youth too.

Ryan, standing still, called her name: **Isabella**, wait.

Isabella continued walking in unfamiliar streets, her tears falling like waterfalls, refusing to stop. She kept remembering all their memories together, questioning why he came back now. The hardest thing a person can endure is waiting.

Chapter Four

Ryan returned by car to **Matthew**'s house and knocked on the door heavily.

Matthew, opening the door: **Ryan**.

Ryan: She told me she doesn't want me, **Matthew**.

Matthew: Calm down, **Ryan**, we'll talk inside. Come on.

Ryan, angrily: How can I calm down? How? I can't calm down without her. I can't. I tried in every way to forget her, but I can't. I can't.

Matthew: Fine, **Ryan**, come in first.

Ryan: Why didn't you tell me about his presence?

Matthew: Whose presence?

Ryan: I saw him. I saw how he looks at her. I saw him looking at her the way I look at her. He sees her with the same gaze, **Matthew**.

Matthew: **Ryan**, I really don't understand.

Ryan, entering the apartment and slamming the door: During my travels, you always told me she no longer loves me. I didn't believe you for a second, but today I did. Why, **Matthew**? Would you believe me if I told you I always wanted to be in your place?

Matthew: My place, how?

Ryan: **Amelia** is much easier than **Isabella**. **Amelia** came back to you easily.

Matthew, angrily: Because I didn't leave her for five years, **Ryan**. What do you want, **Ryan**? You left her alone for five years. She fought everyone for you, even after you left. She stood up to her family for you and refused everyone who tried to get close to her. Did you come now and want her to come back to you easily? You didn't even tell her why you left. I've seen this too much in her. What do you really want? I don't understand you anymore.

Ryan: You're my brother. How can you side with her?

Matthew: **Ryan**, why did you come back?

Ryan: Because this is my homeland. It's natural for me to return.

Matthew: It was your homeland, but it isn't anymore.

Ryan: Why are you talking to me this way?

Matthew: Because I really don't want to continue.

Ryan: Continue what?

Matthew: Continue always standing behind you, even when you're wrong. I always followed you without thinking. Since we were kids, I always took the punishment instead of you. Do you remember? You always got away, and I was punished, even though it was your fault, not mine. I paid the price for all your mistakes, even the mistake of leaving **Isabella**.

Ryan: I didn't know you hid all this inside towards me.

Matthew: There's more inside me, **Ryan**. You've gone too far. Do you want to know the truth? Do you want to know who was looking at **Isabella**?

Ryan, raising his voice: Yes.

Matthew: Fine. It's **William**, **Isabella**'s and **Amelia**'s manager. He has loved **Isabella** since she started working at the lab and has favored her over everyone.

Ryan turned into another person, an angry person who couldn't see ahead, and **Matthew** continued.

Matthew: Do you also remember **Yahya**? He was our friend in school, and you remember well that he loved her. You always prevented that, prevented him from even saying good morning to her. You refused to let him talk to **Amelia** so he wouldn't know about **Isabella**. Since you left, he's been telling **Gabriel** he wants to propose to **Isabella**.

Ryan, as if fire was coming out of his eyes: Are you lying just to hurt me, my friend?

Matthew, with all the calm he could muster: No, it's the truth.

Ryan, defeated by his tears, which began to fall: I will never forget everything you told me now. I will never forget that my only brother hurt me this way. I will never forget the look of hatred I saw today in your eyes.

Matthew closed his eyes, realizing everything he had said in a moment of anger. He opened his eyes, wanting to tell **Ryan** he didn't hate him, that he couldn't hate his brother. Yes, he was very tired, but he didn't want to lose his only friend and brother. He opened his eyes to see that **Ryan** had left.

Matthew, to himself: No, what have I done? Why did I tell him all that?

He rushed to his phone and tried to call **Ryan**, but couldn't reach him.

Matthew, to himself: Come on, **Ryan**, please don't hurt yourself. He closed his eyes, remembering a place he knew **Ryan** had gone to hide.

Matthew, opening his eyes: Yes, he wouldn't go anywhere else.

He took his car and drove to that place. He found **Ryan**'s father's car and saw **Ryan** sitting on a high place, resembling a mountain, standing on its edge.

Matthew: You won't jump, will you?

Ryan, with tears filling his eyes, didn't respond or turn to the voice.

Matthew, approaching him: I knew you were here. Do you remember the first time we came here together? One day, we had a fight at school. It was you and me against five people, and we were all suspended for a whole week. We couldn't go home because our faces showed signs of the fight. When we returned, we saw this place, and since then, we've always come here to hide whenever we had a problem. Do you remember why?

Ryan didn't respond or turn, but his tears continued to fall.

Matthew: Fine, I'll remind you. Because we feel free in this place, we feel like the universe is very small and all problems can be solved no matter how big they are. Every time we came here because of a problem, we didn't leave until we found a solution. I also remember that **Amelia** and **Isabella** knew about this place because we told them about it that same day.

Ryan, finally responding: At that time, none of us knew the meaning of hatred or malice.

He looked at **Matthew** with eyes full of tears: Isn't that right, my friend, my brother?

Matthew: And we're still like that, my brother.

Ryan, smiling: Your brother! Really!

Matthew: **Ryan**, I'm truly sorry for what I said, but...

Ryan: But what? Do you think I'm a fool, **Matthew**? Do you think I don't know how you feel about me?

Matthew: No, **Ryan**.

Ryan: But it's not my fault. I didn't deprive you of family warmth and brotherhood. I didn't make you live a painful past. But I tried and worked hard so you wouldn't feel that lack. I forced my family to treat you as my real brother. I always tried not to make you feel inferior and was the one who would give his life for you. I was the happiest person when **Amelia** told you she loved you.

Matthew, upon hearing **Amelia**'s name: But she's no longer here, brother. Even she is no longer here.

Ryan, wiping his tears and approaching him: Why, what happened?

Matthew, sadly: She hit me with the truth as you are doing now. Fine, it's not your fault or hers, but it's not mine either.

Ryan, patting **Matthew**'s shoulder: **Matthew**, I want you to continue your treatment.

Matthew: But this thing won't be cured, **Ryan**. You don't know what it means to be deprived of family warmth and find yourself alone. A person wounded by their family never heals.

Ryan: But you're not alone. I'm by your side. Have you forgotten that **Ruby**, your sister, is also by your side?

Matthew: No, since she got married and moved abroad, she doesn't talk to me much. I don't remember the last time I heard her voice. She doesn't worry about my matters. At her wedding, she told **Amelia** not to leave me and told you the same, then left me. But I don't know why. Am I someone unworthy of love, so everyone I love leaves me and goes?

Ryan, gripping **Matthew**'s shoulders tightly: Why do you feel that way? I love you, and **Amelia** does too. We won't leave you alone.

Matthew: I apologize, **Ryan**. You don't deserve this from me.

Ryan: No, I've burdened you already, so...

Matthew: So what? **Isabella** still loves you.

Ryan: No, her eyes didn't tell me that.

Matthew: She's just confused, but I know she still loves you.

Ryan: Did **Yahya** really propose to her? How did he dare to do that?

Matthew, smiling: Maybe he forgot what we used to do to him.

Ryan: Since I was young, my father told me I'm his only son and must be strong and stable to protect my sisters. I must think well about everything. I didn't even believe **Diana** traveled for a scholarship.

Matthew, surprised: Did **Diana** really travel?

Ryan: Why didn't you tell me about that?

Matthew: But I didn't know about it.

Ryan: How?

Matthew: Maybe they told me, and I forgot to tell you. Forget about that. Are you still angry with me?

Ryan: No.

Matthew: Okay, what will you do now?

Ryan: I'll look for a job and try again with **Isabella**. You should go back to **Amelia**. I know well she didn't mean to hurt you.

Matthew: No.

Ryan: **Matthew**, **Amelia** loves you. Don't lose her over an angry conversation, or I would have lost you too.

Matthew: I'm very hungry. Let's go to my apartment and order food like old times.

Ryan, hugging him: Okay, let's go, my brother.

Isabella returned to her house to find **Amelia** waiting for her in her room.

Amelia: Where have you been all this time? I was very worried about you.

Isabella, with traces of tears on her eyes: Nothing, I'm fine.

Amelia: **Isabella**, tell me what's going on.

Isabella: I'll tell you. I've made an important decision.

Amelia: What is it?

Isabella: I will agree.

Amelia: Agree to what?

Isabella: **William** or **Yahya**.

Amelia: What? Are you in your right mind?

Isabella: Yes, and I think I'll agree to **William**. I feel he understands me more.

Amelia, placing her hands on **Isabella**'s shoulders: **Isabella**, but that's not a solution. What fault does he have?

Isabella: And what fault do I have? What did I do to deserve all this? I don't know what price I'm paying or for how long, but I'm tired.

Amelia: I'll leave you now to rest a bit, and after you calm down, we'll talk again.

Isabella: **Amelia**, you didn't tell my family, did you?

Amelia: Yes, I told them you only argued with **William**.

Amelia took her bag and left, then turned to **Isabella** again.

Amelia: **William** asked me about **Ryan**.

Isabella: And what did you tell him?

Amelia: Nothing, I told him about your engagement and **Ryan** leaving.

Isabella: All this, and you didn't tell him anything, **Amelia**.

Amelia: I didn't give him details. I'll go now. Don't do anything until you calm down and think well.

Amelia left **Isabella** alone and met **Isabella**'s family outside, telling them that **Isabella** wanted to stay alone for a while because of a problem at work.

Isabella went to her closet, took out a box containing letters, photos, and a dried red rose, and opened the first letter to read it.

Letter: "Now you've turned 17. I wish the days would go by quickly so we could grow up together. I desperately want to see you in a wedding dress, coming to me with your smile that I love, standing next to me as I wear a suit, and we begin our true life together. I eagerly await this day."

A tear fell from her eyes, leaving a mark on the written letter, then she closed it and took out a second letter to read.

Letter: "Today you've turned 16. Today I was afraid of losing you because of the fight that happened. Me and **Matthew** against five people. I didn't care about the suspension for a week; all I cared about was how I would see you during that week? But I don't regret protecting you and I will always be your shadow, as long as I live. But I will be a shadow that doesn't leave you in the dark too."

In a quiet voice, she looked at the letter as if he was there: "But my shadow left me five years ago. Today he came back as if nothing happened, as if he didn't leave me alone to fall and stand, fall and stand again."

She closed it and opened another letter.

Letter: "I know you're used to me writing you a letter on each of your birthdays, so you have it wherever you go. Because I feel the sincerity of my feelings when I write to you with my pen, not just a text sent to your phone. Today you turned 18, but it's really a special day because today we'll get engaged. Today my ring will light up your finger, **Isabella**, do you believe this? Today half our dream will come true, and the other half will come true at our wedding. I feel like I'm flying with joy. All that separates us from this is just a few hours. You will be mine, **Isabella**, after all these attempts. Finally, your family agreed that I become your life partner. Finally, everything is on the right path, the path we always dreamed of."

She closed this letter and started crying again, remembering every second of that day. She found a photo of them. He was wearing a navy-blue suit, looking at her while holding her hand tightly. She was wearing a dark blue dress, her hair blowing freely with two strands covering part of her eyes, laughing a charming laugh. This was always the picture he escaped to during his travels. She didn't know that both of them would see this picture alone and cry about everything that happened.

She talked to herself and said: "Only this picture remains of our photos. I burned the rest. I burned them thinking I burned our memories, but that didn't happen. I couldn't just part with this picture."

We go to **Amelia**, who, as soon as she left **Isabella**, called **Matthew**.

Matthew: Hello.

Amelia: Isn't all this fighting enough? Didn't you miss me at all? I'm sorry, **Matthew**, I didn't want to say all that.

Matthew: Hmm, I'll think about whether to accept your apology or not.

Amelia, smiling: Does that mean the old **Matthew** will return?

Matthew: No, the new **Matthew**. **Ryan** is with me now.

Amelia: Okay, I'll hang up and we'll talk later.

Ryan: **Amelia**, wait. I want to talk to you.

Amelia: Talk to me about what, **Ryan**? You broke her again today.

Ryan: But she didn't tell me that, **Amelia**. She told me she no longer knew someone named **Ryan**.

Amelia: It's not my place to talk about that, but stop hurting her.

Ryan: Hurting her! Do you believe what you're saying, **Amelia**?

Matthew: Okay, guys, I think the conversation should end here. I'll talk to you later, **Amelia**.

Amelia: Did you forgive me?

Matthew: Since when have I ever held a grudge against you? Goodbye.

They hung up, and **Ryan** and **Matthew** sat together, reminiscing all their memories until the conversation turned to **Matthew**'s family again.

Ryan: Do you want to talk about them?

Matthew: I feel ashamed.

Ryan: How?

Matthew: I've never seen parents as selfish as them.

Ryan: But what they did was best for everyone. You know that.

Matthew: I don't know what my fault is. Why do they make me pay for their mistakes? Did they only realize they were incompatible and couldn't live together after my birth?

Ryan: But they endured it for your sake and did raise you.

Matthew: No, **Ryan**, their role shouldn't be limited to just providing money.

Ryan: But they tried in every way.

Matthew, sadly: I remember the day they left me well, as if it was yesterday. It was our last day in high school, and I was so happy. I felt like I really grew up. When I returned home, they told me they were separating and each would continue their life with someone else. It felt like a dagger pierced my heart. How could they leave me alone? All I thought about was my sister, **Ruby**, but at that time, I saw she didn't care. She was preparing for her wedding. Since her wedding, they haven't thought to tell me what happened in their lives or even check on me. I thought, okay, **Ruby** would make up for their absence, but she traveled with her husband. She only talks to me on the phone occasionally. Before she left, she asked you and **Amelia** not to leave me.

Ryan: At that time, I couldn't ask you why you decided to isolate yourself from the rest of your family.

Matthew, even more sadly: Because it's not their role. My parents left me; will someone else care for me?

Ryan: But you know I won't leave you, right?

Matthew, smiling: Since then, I've hated this feeling.

Ryan: What feeling?

Matthew: Feeling pity for me.

Ryan: Are you crazy? I don't pity you. I know you're strong enough to bear all this and overcome it. Fate gives everyone burdens, knowing they can overcome and bear them. It won't give you a load you can't handle. It gives your patience and endurance in proportion to this load, so I trust you.

Matthew: So, you will also overcome all this.

Ryan: About what?

Matthew: **Ryan**, I know you didn't return because you wanted to come back, like when you left because you were forced to.

Ryan: That's true, but the road seems closed in front of me.

Matthew: Tell me, and we'll find a solution. Is he the reason for your return, just like he was the reason for your departure?

Ryan: I'm tired, brother. Why doesn't everything go naturally?

Matthew: **Ryan**, why don't you tell me the matter?

Ryan: I'm going home now, but I want to ask you two things.

Matthew: That means you won't tell me. Fine, but you know I'm always behind you.

Ryan: Of course, I know that.

Matthew: So, what are the two things?

Ryan: Try to get **Amelia** to talk to **Isabella** and ask if she still loves me or not.

Matthew: Why don't you tell her the truth?

Ryan: No, I won't bear anything that hurts her because of me. I agreed to stay away from her as long as she is fine.

Matthew: But she thinks you left on your own accord.

Ryan: **Matthew**, you promised me you wouldn't tell anyone. You didn't tell **Amelia**, did you?

Matthew: No, I didn't tell her, but...

Ryan, interrupting: The second thing is to find me a job at the same company where you work.

Matthew: Really!

Ryan: Did you think I would be jobless?

Matthew: No.

Ryan: I'm going. Goodbye.

Matthew: Goodbye.

After **Ryan** stood up and opened the door, he took a step back, looked at **Matthew**, and said: What happened today won't happen again.

Matthew: Don't worry, my brother.

Ryan: Fine.

Afterwards, **Ryan** left and found his phone ringing with an unknown number while driving his father's car.

Chapter Five

Ryan: Hello.

Caller: Did you forget me?

Ryan: Why are you calling me now?

Caller: I came for you.

Ryan stopped the car.

Ryan: What? What are you doing here?

Caller: Did you think I would leave you that easily?

Ryan: What do you want from me?

Caller: We'll meet tonight.

Ryan: I can't.

Caller: I'm telling you, not asking for your opinion. I'll send you the address in a message. Goodbye.

Ryan: Wait. Hello?

Ryan, to himself: What have I done? This is all I needed.

At exactly 8 PM, **Ryan** went to the address in the message and knocked on the door. A blonde girl opened the door.

Ryan: **Fiona**.

Fiona, hugging him: I missed you so much.

Ryan, stepping back: Why did you come back?

Fiona: Did you forget you are my home? Come inside, let's talk a bit.

Ryan: No, I came to tell you that you need to leave here.

Fiona: Why? Did you go back to her?

Ryan: It's none of your business, **Fiona**.

Fiona, raising her voice: None of my business! Do you come to me when you want and leave when you want and tell me it's none of my business?

Ryan: I think your voice is getting louder.

Fiona, calming down: Will you keep standing outside like this?

Ryan: Fine, put on a jacket, and let's go out together.

Fiona: Wait a minute.

During that minute, **Ryan** sent a message to **Isabella** saying: "You haven't changed much since the last time. You're still that girl I left, still crying over everything. I never forgot you, **Isabella**. I want you to know one thing: I didn't leave you by my own will."

He sighed, looking at the sky, then back at the phone, seeing she read the message but had blocked him, affirming that he didn't matter to her anymore. He looked at the phone with sadness and found **Fiona** standing behind him.

Fiona: Let's go.

Ryan: Wait.

Fiona: Don't tell me you're not coming.

Ryan: No, everything is gone. It doesn't matter to me anymore. There's no other girl in my life but you.

Fiona, happily: Does that mean you won't go back to her?

Ryan: Let's go.

They went together, then **Ryan** stopped the car.

Fiona: Why did you stop?

Ryan: Do you mind if we stay here a bit? I want to breathe.

He got out of the car, looked up at the sky, inhaled the air, and closed his eyes. **Fiona** also got out and stood next to him.

Fiona: Will you tell me?

Ryan, still with his eyes closed: I don't want to talk.

Fiona, imitating him, closing her eyes: Fine, as you wish.

They stayed like that until **Ryan** broke the silence, saying: Have you ever felt that something is missing?

Fiona: Something like what?

Ryan: I don't know, but I feel that something is missing. Maybe an old dream, maybe a part of me, maybe myself.

Fiona: Is she the missing part of you?

Ryan, opening his eyes: I realized today that everything is over, **Fiona**. I know you don't like me talking about her.

Fiona: No, because she's your past, and usually, people can't escape their past. But I'm not your past; I'm your present and future.

Ryan: Do you really think that?

Fiona: **Ryan**, I came today just for you.

Ryan: Every time I felt I was about to give up, I found you by my side. I won't forget that, **Fiona**, and I will always do that.

They continued talking like that. When they finished, **Ryan** took her back to her place and then returned home and slept.

The next morning, **William**'s room door was knocked.

William: Come in.

Isabella: Can I talk to you for a bit?

William, closing his laptop: Of course, come in.

Isabella: Look, I want to consult you about something.

William: Are you going to ask me if you should go back to him or not?

Isabella: Yes, I want to know your opinion.

William: Look, **Isabella**, this is something that doesn't concern anyone else. It's your decision. Moreover, I don't know everything that happened in the past to think properly.

Isabella: Okay, I'll tell you if you don't mind.

William nodded in agreement.

Isabella: **Amelia**, **Matthew**, he and I grew up together. We studied in the same school, but **Matthew** and **Ryan** are older than **Amelia** and me. Since I was born, I always saw him by my side, never separated from me. When he was in high school, he proposed to me, but my family didn't agree because we were too young. After I reached high school, he proposed again. Initially, my family didn't agree, but after I insisted, they agreed on the condition that I wouldn't neglect my studies and the marriage would take place after I finished university. We got engaged, but after four months, he changed as if he became a different person. I didn't know why. He refused to tell me the reason. Whenever I talked to him, he made excuses and distanced himself from me. I even imagined he never loved me from the beginning and was lying to me. In the fifth month of our engagement, he asked to meet me outside. When we met, he told me he was leaving the country and wouldn't return, and I shouldn't wait for him. On the same day, **Matthew** did the same with **Amelia** and left her. They both traveled.

Her eyes filled with tears as she continued.

Isabella: At that time, **Amelia** and I were shattered. We didn't know the reason they left the country like that. But after three months, **Matthew** returned to **Amelia** and told me **Ryan** wouldn't return.

William, handing her a tissue: I understand. You don't need to continue.

Isabella: I don't want to go back to him, but...

William: But you want to understand why he did that. All your memories with him tell you to give him another chance.

Isabella, surprised: How did you know I would say that?

William: Maybe because I went through the same thing, so I feel you.

Isabella: What happened? Did your girlfriend leave you?

William: If you want my opinion, ask him why he left you, then decide what you want. But don't leave before telling him everything inside you, so you don't regret it later.

He continued sadly: If you keep your words and feelings inside, there will come a time when you'll feel like a stone is settled on your heart, making it hard to breathe.

Isabella: **William**, what's this mystery? Tell me what happened.

William, opening his laptop: Nothing.

Isabella, standing to leave the room: Okay, as you wish. I won't delay you any longer. If you want to tell me, I'll surely listen to you.

William, closing his eyes and saying: I loved her so much. I didn't expect to love someone as much as I loved her. I loved her more than myself. We studied together in the same college and the same department.

Isabella stopped and looked at him.

William continued: I fulfilled all her wishes. Even if she asked for a star from the sky, I would have brought it to her.

Isabella: What happened after that?

William: Everything was going well until graduation day. I promised her I would tell my family about everything.

Isabella: Did your family not agree?

William: I wished that had happened, but what really happened was that the day after graduation, she didn't respond to any of my calls. I had a friend—no, not my friend, my brother—I thought he was my brother. I called him to tell him what happened, thinking he might know how to reach her. He said he would try. A week later, I saw her picture wearing an engagement dress, standing next to my friend whom I considered my brother. Above the picture, it said, "A dream of years realized today."

Isabella, approaching him: How could they do this to you?

William: They were the two closest people to me and my heart. I always trusted no one else but them.

Isabella: What did you do?

William, his eyes filled with tears: I couldn't confront them. I couldn't ask them why.

Isabella: Maybe he didn't know you loved her.

William: No, every time we argued, he always listened to us and fixed everything between us. He knew I loved her more than anything.

Isabella: And then you decided to make everything just right. Is that correct?

William: Correct. After that, I got very sick and distanced myself from everything. I couldn't even block them on Facebook. I wanted them to stay visible to me. Whenever I felt weak, I would see them and get stronger again. I worked with my father here, then I took over the work. He sent me a message saying, "I want you to share our joy. You are my brother. I want you by my side." He sent me the location and time of the wedding.

Isabella: Did you go?

William: Yes, I went. That was the last day I felt weak. After that day, I became stronger and more mature. She didn't deserve my love. Maybe I was too much for her. I saw her beside him wearing the dress she always dreamed of wearing next to me.

Isabella: How didn't they feel they betrayed you?

William: I told you; I couldn't ask them.

Isabella: What happened after that?

William: Nothing. I became the **William** you see now. I decided to make everything just right—work, sadness, joy, and even love.

Isabella: I understand everything now.

William: That's why I tell you to confront him. Only confrontation will heal you. Painkillers and escaping will only ease your pain temporarily. They won't remove it. They will make you feel better for a short period. The solution is to face your sadness and fear. Confrontation is more painful, but it will heal you forever. Be sure that everything will pass. Even sadness will pass. Life will continue. It won't stop for someone. No one will die because of separation. We imagine that and give things more weight than they deserve.

Isabella: I apologize.

William: For what?

Isabella: For making you remember all this because of me.

William: But I didn't forget to remember it, **Isabella**. But I have healed. This story turned me into a better person.

Isabella: Did you meet a girl you loved after that?

William, smiling: **Isabella**, what do you want?

Isabella, also smiling: Nothing. Just asking a passing question.

William: Okay, go back to work.

Isabella: Does that mean you met someone?

William: **Isabella**.

Isabella: What?

William: Go to work.

Isabella: Okay, but remember you didn't tell me everything.

Isabella left the room, and **William** smiled, looking at her, then continued his work. At the same time, at **Ryan**'s house, he received a message.

Message: Will we meet today too?

Ryan read it and smiled, replying: I knew you wouldn't leave me alone. Fine, we'll meet, but I'll go to **Matthew** first.

Fiona: Give me your address, and we'll meet there.

Ryan sent a message to **Fiona**: "What, are you crazy?"

Fiona: Come on, send me your location.

Ryan closed the phone, got into the car, and went to **Matthew**'s workplace, knocking on **Matthew**'s office door.

Matthew: Come in.

Ryan: How are you, brother?

Matthew: **Ryan**, why are you here?

Ryan: Did you forget your promise to me?

Matthew: No, no, I didn't forget.

Ryan: I know your break is about to start, so I came so we could talk.

Matthew: Okay, let's go out and sit somewhere quiet.

They went out together and sat in a quiet place.

Matthew: Come on, talk.

Ryan: Talk about what?

Matthew: **Ryan**, I understand you from your eyes.

Ryan: She blocked me yesterday.

Matthew: What?

Ryan: I sent her a message. She read it and then blocked me. **Matthew**, I don't understand her anymore.

Matthew: **Ryan**, do you want to talk about the facts?

Ryan: Yes.

Matthew: But you won't get angry.

Ryan: Talk, **Matthew**.

Matthew: Okay, but you will tell me the truth.

Ryan: **Matthew**.

Matthew: What do you want, **Ryan**? Do you really love her, or are you just used to her presence?

Ryan: What? Do you believe what you're saying? You, more than anyone...

Matthew, interrupting: More than anyone knows what you did for her. That's what you were going to say, right?

Ryan: Yes, **Matthew**, how can you ask me such a question?

Matthew: That was in the past, **Ryan**. All those sacrifices were in the past, but now I see two completely different people, you and her. Both of you have changed a lot. The old **Isabella** is no longer in front of you, **Ryan**. She has grown and changed, and so have you. You both continued life without each other, so life will continue without her and without you.

Ryan: **Matthew**, I haven't loved anyone and won't love anyone but **Isabella**.

Matthew: You've exhausted her so much. Leave her.

Ryan: Leave her, how? I still love her, but I don't know if she still loves me or not. Besides, **Fiona** came.

Matthew: **Fiona**! How did she come?

Ryan: She came here for me.

Matthew: In astonishment, **Fiona** is here!

Ryan: I was as surprised as you are.

Matthew: What will you do now?

Ryan: You know?

Matthew: What?

Ryan: Every time I fell, **Fiona** was beside me. She never left me alone abroad.

Matthew: I don't really understand you. A minute ago, you were telling me you still love **Isabella**, and now you're talking about **Fiona**.

Ryan: Yes, I don't know.

Matthew: **Ryan**, what do you want?

Ryan: I don't know, but **Isabella** means everything to me.

Matthew: What about **Fiona**? I've seen her with you before, and she's willing to do anything just to see you happy.

Ryan: Yes, I remember that. I always went to her to talk about **Isabella**, and she still listens to me and comforts me in every way.

Matthew: Do you want to hurt two girls?

Ryan: No, not at all. **Fiona** knows the truth and knows everything, but the thing I don't understand is why she accepts this situation.

Matthew: Maybe because she loves you?

Ryan: **Fiona** loves me? No, you've misunderstood a lot.

Matthew, laughing: Of course, that's why she came now to tell you.

Fiona, approaching them: **Matthew**, how are you?

Matthew shook her hand and said: Fine, and you?

Fiona, sitting next to **Ryan**: What's funny, **Matthew**?

Matthew: I won't ask how you knew our place because he definitely sent you, our location. But are you still following him everywhere?

Ryan: Yes, I sent her the location. What do you want now?

Matthew, laughing: Nothing. I'll go back to work and leave you two to talk. **Matthew** left, and **Ryan** and **Fiona** talked.

Ryan: I didn't know you would get here so easily.

Fiona: You sent me the location. Why would it be hard to get here? Come on, order me some food. I'm very hungry.

Ryan: Excuse me.

His phone rang at that second. He looked at it and found it was an unknown number.

Ryan: Hello.

Caller: Brother.

Chapter Six

Caller: Brother.

Ryan: **Diana**, where are you?

Diana: I missed you so much, brother.

Ryan, angrily: Where are you? How did you not tell me about your travel?

Diana: It happened suddenly, so I couldn't tell you.

Ryan, still angry: How did it happen suddenly?

Diana: My marriage happened unexpectedly.

Ryan, standing: What? **Diana**, did you get married? When and how? Didn't you go abroad for a study mission?

Diana: Is that what they told you?

Ryan, raising his voice: **Diana**, how did you get married without my knowledge, and when?

Fiona, talking to him: Is that your sister?

Ryan, looking at **Fiona**: Not now, **Fiona**.

He continued talking to **Diana** on the phone.

Ryan: Come on, I'm waiting for an answer. How and when did this happen?

Diana: I have to hang up now. I'll call you later.

Ryan: **Diana**, wait, don't hang up. **Diana**!

Diana hung up, leaving **Ryan** with a thousand questions swirling inside him.

Fiona: What happened?

Ryan, standing: I need to go home now.

Fiona: Okay, wait for me.

Ryan: I don't have time, **Fiona**. I need to go home.

Ryan returned home angrily and found his parents.

Eleanor: You're back early.

Ryan, raising his voice: Why didn't you tell me?

Eleanor: Tell you what?

Ryan: What! I think you need to tell me why **Diana** traveled.

Eleanor remained silent, and **Patrick** came out of his room at the sound of **Ryan**'s voice.

Patrick: What's going on, **Ryan**?

Ryan: Come on, Mom, I'm waiting for your answer. Why did my sister travel?

Patrick: We told you what happened.

Ryan: Is that the truth, Dad? Well, **Diana** called me and told me she got married. Why didn't you tell me?

Eleanor, crying: Yes, she got married and traveled.

Ryan: Why didn't you tell me that? And whom did she marry?

Eleanor: What do you think? She surprised us too.

Ryan: How?

Eleanor began to explain, taking us back to that time on a Monday. We see **Diana** returning from work, approaching **Eleanor** and saying:

Diana: Mom, I want to tell you something.

Eleanor: How was your day at work?

Diana: I'll tell you. There's someone who wants to meet you and Dad.

Eleanor, smiling: Does he want to marry you?

Diana: Yes, Mom. I love him very much.

Eleanor: But...

Diana: But I'm a year older than him, just one year.

Eleanor: **Diana**, are you joking with me?

Diana: No, I'm not joking.

Eleanor: Do you want to marry someone younger than you?

Diana: It's just one year, Mom. No one will notice. Please, give him a chance. Nothing will happen.

Eleanor: When did you meet him?

Diana: I met him at work, Mom. But please, try to convince Dad.

Eleanor: I'm not convinced, but fine, I'll talk to **Patrick**, and we'll sit and talk with him.

Diana: Okay, I'll arrange a meeting.

Eleanor: What's his name?

Diana: **Victor**.

A week later, **Victor** met **Eleanor** and **Patrick**.

Victor: **Diana** told me a lot about you, and I wanted to meet you.

Patrick: Well, Mr. **Victor**, but I'd like to know more about you.

Victor: Without the 'Mr.' is better. Sure, I'll tell you everything about me. I've been working in this field for quite a while, but I learn quickly, so I progress fast in my job. Two months ago, **Diana** came to work, and I noticed her. I got to know her and wanted to meet her family to put her heart at ease. So, I told her to tell you.

Patrick: I think you know that these things don't happen quickly. It takes time to get to know you, and you to know us. But what **Eleanor**, my wife, told me is that **Diana** is a year older than you.

Victor: Yes, that's true, but I don't think it's an obstacle between us.

Patrick: It's not an obstacle, but will you agree to marry a girl older than you?

Victor: It's just one year. No one will notice.

Eleanor: That's exactly what **Diana** said.

Victor: Yes, **Diana** and I think alike, and I think that's what made me notice her initially.

Patrick: No one will notice, I agree with you. But what about you?

Victor: I don't understand.

Patrick: You know she's older than you, and she knows that too.

Victor, slightly angry: But I said...

Seeing **Patrick** and **Eleanor** looking at him, he realized his mistake.

Calming his voice, he continued: I didn't mean that, but it's just one year.

After two hours, the meeting ended, and **Patrick** and **Eleanor** returned home to find **Diana** waiting for them.

Diana: What happened?

Patrick: What happened, **Diana**?

Diana: That's my question, Dad.

Patrick: We'll sit and talk first, **Eleanor** and I.

Diana: Okay, what's your initial opinion of him?

Patrick: **Eleanor**, I'm in the room.

Eleanor: I'll come now.

Patrick walked towards the room.

Eleanor: **Diana**, I want you to calm down a bit.

Diana: What happened, Mom?

Eleanor: Nothing, but I don't want you to hope too much.

Diana, sadly: Why?

Eleanor: I'll talk to your father and tell you.

Eleanor went to the room.

Patrick: Close the door.

Eleanor, closing the door: So, what's your decision?

Patrick: I don't know, but I'm not comfortable with him.

Eleanor: My heart tells me trouble will come from him, but **Diana** is attached to him.

Patrick: What's the use of attachment, **Eleanor**? Should we give our daughter to someone untrustworthy? I'll investigate him.

Eleanor: Will you tell **Ryan**?

Patrick: No, we won't do that. **Ryan** is alone in a country that's not his and doesn't belong to him.

Eleanor: My heart aches because of his absence. Since the last call, I feel he's not the same.

Patrick: They've grown up, **Eleanor**, and each one is responsible for themselves now. Let him learn on his own. He chose to leave.

We move forward a month in time.

Eleanor: Shouldn't we tell **Ryan** about **Diana**'s engagement?

Patrick: When will we tell him? Will he come if we tell him?

Eleanor: At least he will know that today is **Diana**'s engagement.

Patrick: Everything happened quickly, **Eleanor**. We'll tell him for sure, but not now.

Back to the present, **Ryan** listened to this story in astonishment.

Ryan: Why didn't you tell me at that time?

Patrick: There was no time. Everything happened quickly.

Ryan: What happened after that?

Patrick: Nothing. A week after the engagement, **Victor** decided to get married. After that, he told us he would travel and wanted **Diana** to go with him.

Ryan: Why did you agree to this marriage?

Patrick: I investigated him and found he was suitable.

Ryan: Suitable how? If he wanted her so much, why did he make her leave the country and leave us?

Patrick: Leave us? I think you forgot you returned recently.

Ryan: No, I didn't forget, but I don't believe this story at all.

Patrick: Would I leave my daughter with someone unsuitable?

Ryan: Mom, why are you silent now?

Eleanor, crying: What do you want to hear, **Ryan**?

Ryan: The truth. I want to hear the truth, Mom.

Eleanor: This is the truth.

Ryan: Yes, I know. I've heard that line before.

Ryan left the room and went to his own room.

Hana came to his room and said: Do you really want to know the truth, brother?

Ryan walked toward her and patted her shoulders: Yes, what happened?

Hana: I want everything to go back to the way it was, **Ryan**, but I'm scared.

Ryan: What are you scared of, **Hana**? I'm back with you. Tell me the truth.

Hana: I'm scared for **Diana**, **Ryan**.

She closed her eyes tightly, as if remembering a scene, then opened them, tears falling.

Ryan, hugging her: **Hana**, I'm worried. What happened? Why are you worried about **Diana**?

Hana: From the beginning, I knew he wasn't suitable for **Diana**. I always told her not to take this step, but she didn't listen to me. I even told her to consult you about it, but she...

Ryan: **Hana**, calm down a bit and sit.

Hana sat on the couch and tried to stop her tears.

Ryan: Come on, tell me.

Hana: The truth is that since **Victor** entered **Diana**'s life, everything changed for the worse. I don't know why she follows him in everything. She doesn't even think if he's lying or not. Since their engagement, she's always arguing with Dad, Mom, and me. I feel like he's making her distance herself from us.

Ryan: Calm down. Why did everything happen so quickly, and why did Dad agree for **Diana** to leave?

Hana: At first, **Victor** showed that he was kind and gentle, but after the engagement, he turned into another person. He always told Dad he wanted to hasten the marriage because of his busy work schedule and wanted **Diana** to travel with him.

Ryan: Is that all?

Hana: One day, he was talking to **Diana** on the phone, arguing with her. I heard his voice and saw her crying; afraid he would leave her.

She closed her eyes, remembering the same scene, wanting to tell **Ryan** but feeling like the words were stuck in her throat.

Ryan: Okay, **Hana**, that's enough. But if anything happens from now on, please come and tell me. No matter what, don't be afraid of anything as long as I'm alive.

Ryan left her, stood, and went to leave the room.

Hana: **Ryan**.

Ryan, turning to her: Did you remember anything else?

Hana: Why did you leave us and go? Why did you leave **Isabella**, **Ryan**? She doesn't deserve this from you.

Ryan looked at her sadly, then left. **Hana** remembered everything and cried alone.

Ryan, on the phone: Where are you?

Matthew: I'm going home now. What happened, did you argue with **Fiona**?

Ryan: I want to talk to you. I'll come to you.

Matthew: **Ryan**, are you okay?

Ryan: We'll talk when I get there.

An hour later, **Ryan** knocked on **Matthew**'s door. He opened it.

Matthew, opening the door: What happened?

Ryan: How do you not know that **Diana** got married?

Matthew: She got married? When?

Ryan, entering the house and closing the door behind him: I don't know. She talked to me on the phone and said she got married. My parents told me a story I didn't believe.

Matthew: But I didn't know any of this. I wasn't even aware she traveled.

Ryan: How? When we were abroad together and you decided to return, I told you to take care of my family and tell me everything happening with them.

Matthew: That's true, and I did that. But they didn't tell me this part, so I didn't tell you.

Ryan: Since I returned, everything has gone against my wishes. Everything is ruined, **Matthew**. Why is this happening to me? And how will I solve this problem when they didn't tell me the truth? **Hana** told me she's very worried about **Diana**.

Matthew: First, you need to calm down to think properly. Sit down, and I'll get you a glass of water.

Matthew got him a glass of water and handed it to him.

Ryan: **Matthew**, do you know his name?

Matthew: **Victor**.

Ryan: I want his full name, **Matthew**.

Ryan: I don't know, but he worked with her, and she's a year older than him.

Matthew: That's not enough information.

Ryan, looking at **Matthew**: I want to ask you another favor.

Matthew: What?

Ryan: Send a message to **Amelia** and have her send it to **Isabella**.

Matthew: Why don't you send it to her yourself?

Ryan looked at the ground sadly and remained silent. **Matthew** continued.

Matthew: Oh yes, I remember. She blocked you.

Ryan: Yes.

Matthew: Okay, how about I send the message to her directly, not to **Amelia**?

Ryan: What difference will it make?

Matthew, to himself: **Amelia** won't send the message.

Ryan: What did you say?

Matthew: It will reach her faster. What do you think?

Ryan: Okay, I agree. Here, give me your phone. She won't block you too, right?

Matthew, handing him the phone: I don't know. We'll try our luck this time.

Ryan took the phone, moved toward the balcony, looked at the phone, and wrote to her:

"**Isabella**, I am **Ryan**. I really need you during this period. I have nothing left. I want you by my side. Leave everything behind now. I promise, after these problems pass, I will give you a full chance to think again about us. I want to meet to talk with you, and this time I won't talk about us. I want to run to you as I used to before. Do you remember? Whenever I went through a tough time, I ran to you, and you always listened to me. Here I am running to you again. Will you allow me to listen to me once more?"

He kept looking at the phone every minute, even every second, to see if she had seen the message.

After half an hour, **Matthew** approached him.

Matthew: Did she say anything?

Ryan: I sent her the message half an hour ago, and she hasn't seen it yet. When does she finish her work?

Matthew: But **Amelia** and **Isabella**'s work hours ended more than two hours ago.

Ryan: More than two hours!

Matthew: Give me the phone. I'll talk to **Amelia** and try to find out where **Isabella** is.

Ryan gave him the phone. **Matthew** called **Amelia**, and she answered.

Matthew: **Amelia**, how are you?

Amelia: Did you really remember me now? Since he returned, you've forgotten to check on me.

Matthew looked at **Ryan** and then stepped away a little.

Matthew: This isn't the time, **Amelia**. Where is **Isabella**?

Amelia: This isn't the time? Did you call to know where **Isabella** is? Is this a request from him?

Matthew: **Amelia**, what's with this tone? All I want to know from you is where **Isabella** is, then we'll talk again freely, you and I.

Amelia: We won't talk, **Matthew**. As for **Isabella**, I think she went with **William**.

Matthew, looking at **Ryan** and then closing his eyes: What? Do they go out together every day?

Amelia: I told you before, he loves her and deserves her. Even **Yahya** deserves her more than **Ryan**.

Matthew: **Amelia**, don't make me angry.

Amelia: Yes, yes, of course, you'll get angry because I talk about him like this.

Matthew: **Amelia**, hang up.

Amelia: Okay, **Matthew**, as you wish.

Matthew hung up with **Amelia** and moved toward **Ryan**.

Ryan: So, where is she?

Matthew: I don't know. **Amelia** told me **Isabella** went.

Ryan: Went where and with whom?

Matthew: I think she wanted to get some fresh air alone. Leave her for now, and when she responds, I'll tell you.

Ryan: Okay, **Matthew**, I'll go now.

Matthew: **Ryan**, what will we do about **Diana**'s problem?

Ryan: I'll try to ask **Hana** to tell me where **Diana** worked and ask her for his full name, and I'll inform you.

Matthew: Okay, what will you do now?

Ryan: I want to see **Fiona**. I got angry at her when **Diana** was talking to me and left her. I'll try to make it up to her.

Matthew: Okay, as you wish.

Ryan left. **Matthew** took a deep breath, then let it out and talked to himself: What will I do now?

Ryan, after leaving **Matthew**'s house, called **Fiona**.

Fiona: Did you remember something?

Ryan, calmly: **Fiona**, I'm really sorry. I know I got very angry at you. So, I'll come to you now, and we'll go to a place I love very much.

Fiona: No, I'm not...

Ryan: Come on, get ready now. I'll reach you soon.

Fiona: But...

He hung up the call, and **Fiona** was happy, standing to get ready. An hour later, **Ryan** went to her, finding her waiting for him outside the building.

Ryan: Why didn't you wait for me inside?

Fiona: I was afraid you'd come and find I wasn't waiting for you, and you'd change your mind.

Ryan: Wait, you look beautiful in this dress.

Fiona: Do you remember it?

Ryan, smiling: Yes, I remember. It was my first gift to you, but the dress became beautiful when you wore it.

Fiona: It was the first time we met, and you were in such a bad state that you didn't feel anything around you because of your anger. When I moved in front of you...

Ryan, laughing: When you moved in front of me suddenly, I spilled some juice on the dress you were wearing. I saw you turn into another girl and insult me.

We go back in time to this scene and moment. We see **Matthew** and **Ryan** in a noisy, crowded place.

Matthew: Enough, **Ryan**, stop these memories.

Ryan: But I miss her so much, brother.

Matthew: We left the country just a month ago, **Ryan**.

Ryan: A month! I haven't heard her voice or seen her for even a minute. Do you believe this?

Matthew: **Ryan**, please stop remembering and talking about her. You wanted this, not her, so you shouldn't be in this state.

Ryan: No, leave me.

Ryan grabbed the cup in front of him, then suddenly turned to find a girl wearing a slightly short black dress moving in front of him, losing his balance and spilling some juice on the girl's dress.

Fiona: Are you blind?

Matthew to **Fiona**: Sorry.

He looked at **Ryan** and said: **Ryan**, let's go.

Ryan, closing his eyes, not knowing what to say: I miss her.

Fiona: What?

Matthew: I really apologize to you.

Fiona: Fine, I'll accept your apology.

She extended her hand and shook **Matthew**'s, saying: My name is **Fiona**.

Matthew, shaking her hand: And I'm **Matthew**, and he is...

Fiona, laughing: **Ryan**, I figured out when I talked to him.

Matthew: Okay, sorry again. We'll go now. Goodbye.

That day ended, and the next day came. **Matthew** and **Ryan** went to the same place, looking for **Fiona**. **Ryan** carried a bag with a dress inside.

Ryan: So, where is she?

Matthew, looking for her: I don't know. Wait, **Ryan**, there she is.

They went to her. **Fiona** looked at **Ryan** and then smiled.

Fiona: You look well today.

Ryan looked at her in astonishment.

Matthew: I'll leave you two alone.

He looked at **Ryan** and said: **Ryan**.

Ryan: Okay, **Matthew**, don't worry. I won't spill anything on anyone like I did yesterday.

Matthew: Fine, I'll sit over there. If you need anything, just wave.

Fiona: So, you won't repeat it?

Ryan, smiling: Yes, I won't repeat it. I won't find a girl like you every day who will overlook what happened.

Fiona: But I overlooked it because you both seemed kind.

Ryan: That's why I brought you this small gift.

Fiona opened the bag and found a long black dress.

Fiona: What's this?

Ryan: I wanted to bring you another dress instead of the one I spilled the drink on yesterday. You know that here, I'll only find dresses open from all sides.

Fiona, laughing: Yes, but this one is long.

Ryan: Yes, I thought you'd like it because I searched everywhere for a long dress. But if you don't like it, I'll return it.

Fiona: Are you kidding? This is the best dress I've seen. Thank you. But how did you know my size when yesterday you weren't aware of anything around you?

Ryan: **Matthew** helped me because he remembered you.

Fiona: Thank you. So, tell me, come on.

Ryan: Tell you what?

Fiona: About the girl who made you reach this state.

Ryan: Okay, I'll tell you.

We return to the present. **Ryan** and **Fiona** smiled, remembering this memory. **Ryan** said to her:

Ryan: Since then, you haven't left me alone, even when **Matthew** returned and left me.

Fiona: I won't leave you, **Ryan**, that's a promise. But I fear you'll leave me.

Ryan, looking at the car: Come on, we'll go to a place I love very much.

They both got in the car. Meanwhile, **Isabella** and **William** were sitting in a quiet place.

William: Why did you choose this place specifically?

Isabella, smiling: Because I love this place, and the food is delicious.

William: **Isabella**, do you want to talk?

Isabella: I want to be silent tonight. Do you mind?

William: No.

Then **Isabella** looked at her phone and found two messages from **Matthew**, puzzled. She opened and read them, finding one from **Ryan** and another from **Matthew** saying:

"**Isabella**, I'm **Matthew**. **Ryan** really needs you. Leave everything that happened between you. This is **Ryan**, **Isabella**. Let's assume you really got over your love for each other, but I doubt that. Stand by him as if he's just someone you grew up with, like a brother. Please, **Isabella**."

She was affected by the messages, not understanding what happened or what problem he was facing. She kept looking at the phone.

William: **Isabella**, are you okay?

Isabella: Yes, yes, I'm fine.

William: Did something happen?

Isabella, closing the phone and holding back her tears: No, nothing happened.

She wondered what to do now. Should she meet him and stand by him, or was it a trap to make her return to him?

She raised her eyes to find him entering the same place where she was sitting, with a girl beside him wearing a long black dress, her hair falling on both shoulders. **Isabella** looked at them intently, then closed her eyes and opened them again to see them standing and heading to sit somewhere.

William: **Isabella**, what happened?

William looked at what **Isabella** was looking at. He remembered it was **Ryan**, then looked at **Isabella** and saw how she looked at **Ryan** in astonishment. **Isabella** and **William** stood up.

William: **Isabella**, calm down.

Isabella walked toward them, then looked at **Ryan** and said: Is this really the big problem you're facing and need me to stand by you to pass?

Ryan raised his eyes, finding her with her voice, and looked at her in astonishment.

Ryan: **Isabella**, it's not what you think.

Fiona stood up: **Isabella**, is this **Isabella**?

Ryan, standing: **Isabella**, listen to me.

William, looking at **Isabella**: **Isabella**, come on, let's go.

Ryan: Is what I'm seeing real?

He continued in anger: How can you go out with him? How?

Chapter Seven

Ryan: Is this the work you're really doing? And above all, you come and ask me if this is the problem I'm facing.

Isabella: Yes, but I'm the naive one, not you. Naive enough to believe you really need me, but clearly, it was a lie and you're living your life normally.

Ryan, sarcastically: Really? And what you're doing is called what?

William to **Ryan**: Enough, I won't tolerate you talking to her like that.

Ryan: What's it to you? She and I are talking.

William: But...

Isabella held his hand and said to **Ryan**: No, it's his business, **Ryan**, because I'll become his fiancée.

William and **Ryan** looked at her. **Fiona** broke her silence and said: Well, what's our business then?

Ryan laughed: Really? Then congratulations to you both. I promise I'll attend your engagement.

He looked at **Fiona** and said: Come on, **Fiona**, we'll leave and let the groom talk to his fiancée alone about their engagement.

Ryan left with **Fiona**, his inner fire burning, the air doing nothing but increasing it.

Fiona, looking at him: Are you okay?

But she got no answer from **Ryan**, not even a reaction.

Ryan walked, remembering his engagement day with **Isabella** and how happy they were then. Was she really with another person now, or did she say that as a reaction to seeing **Fiona** beside him? But everything she did since his return confirmed she had indeed moved on and no longer wanted him.

William, breaking the silence: My mind tells me to stay quiet, but I can't. How can you tell him I'll become your fiancé? I don't remember ever saying this to you.

Isabella, her eyes filled with tears, said in a low voice: I know, but...

William, interrupting her loudly: But what, **Isabella**? I told you everything before and said I want everything to be just right. Do you really want me to get engaged to a girl who is still thinking about her ex-fiancé?

Isabella, crying and raising her voice: So, what do you want from me? Why do you stay with me all the time during work and outside work? I never lied to you, and I don't want to take this step. But I said it to him because...

William: To make him jealous, to upset him as you were upset seeing a girl next to him. I understand that, but what's my role in this?

Isabella: Okay, I apologize. I thought you'd support me.

William, raising his voice more, attracting everyone's attention: But I supported you, **Isabella**. Anyone else would have left, but I didn't.

An employee approached them: Please lower your voices or leave the place.

William: Fine, I'll pay the bill and go.

He paid the bill and looked at **Isabella**.

William: Come on, I'll take you home.

Isabella went far from **William**'s car.

William: Where are you going? The car is here. **Isabella**, I'm talking to you.

William got into the car and drove slowly behind **Isabella**, opening the window.

William: **Isabella**, come on, get in.

Isabella: Leave me alone. I want to be alone.

William: Come on, **Isabella**, I'm not talking to a little girl to be stubborn.

Isabella: Go away. I don't want you.

William: **Isabella**, get in the car.

Isabella, looking at him: No.

William: **Isabella**, fine, look at me.

Isabella, stopping: What? What do you want?

William: Get in, we'll talk in the car. Come on, **Isabella**, I won't let you walk all this way alone.

Isabella got in and said: But I won't talk to you.

William, laughing: Okay, as you wish, my fiancée.

Isabella: I'm not your fiancée, and I'll resign tomorrow.

William: We'll see about that.

Isabella: I won't talk to you. I want to go home now.

Switching to **Fiona** and **Ryan**. **Ryan** dropped **Fiona** at home and drove aimlessly through the streets, remembering **Isabella** standing there with **William** behind her. He remembered how she held **William**'s hand, telling him he would be her fiancé and had the right to intervene.

Ryan returned home after two hours of walking alone in the streets. He heard loud voices from inside the apartment and rushed in, worried.

Hana: But this is my future.

Patrick: Isn't what happened with **Diana** and **Ryan** enough?

Hana: It's not my fault. Why make me pay for their mistakes?

Eleanor, sitting on the couch: What did I do to deserve all this pain? Was it written that I should live with the agony of losing my children while they're still alive?

Ryan: What's happening?

Patrick: Nothing. Don't interfere.

Ryan: How can I not interfere? She's my little sister.

Patrick: Really? You remember your responsibility towards your siblings now? Is this what I raised you to be?

Ryan: What's happening, Dad? Since I returned, you haven't let me interfere in anything related to them. Whenever I talk, you tell me I left you and went away.

Patrick, looking at **Hana**: **Hana**, I gave my final decision on this matter. There's no room for discussion.

Hana: But what's my fault? Why should I pay the price?

Patrick left, followed by **Eleanor**, both trying to hold back their tears until they reached their room and closed the door.

Eleanor, patting her husband **Patrick** on the shoulder.

Patrick: I know it's not her fault, but...

Eleanor: But what? You've controlled everything related to **Hana** and **Diana** after **Ryan** left so they wouldn't follow his path. When **Diana** left, you controlled **Hana** even more, intervening in her workplace, making sure it was on the next street from where we live.

Patrick: Do you want them all to leave us? Is this your motherhood? Isn't it enough that you failed to raise them properly, making them never listen to me? You made each one decide and do what they want. This is the result of your upbringing.

Eleanor: Really! And where were you when I raised them? Yes, I did all this because I didn't want them to be like me, saying yes and okay only. I wanted each one to be in control of their decisions and destiny, not like me, controlled by my father in everything. When I married you, you did the same. That's why you chose me, not out of love but to impose your control over me.

Patrick: Yes, not out of love. I didn't love anyone but her.

Eleanor: After all these years, after everything that happened between you and her, after everything I did for you, you stand in front of me now and tell me you still love her! Wasn't it enough that you named my daughter after her (**Diana**)? Do you think I'm a fool and believed you only loved the name? I knew you refused **Victor** because you didn't want anyone to take **Diana** from you.

Patrick: But I didn't know I was such a traitor in your eyes. Who's the real traitor? The one who betrayed her lifelong friend, whom she always called her sister?

Eleanor, raising her voice: Yes, me. But do you remember how many times I brought you two together? Do you remember her family didn't want you? You called me, crying, saying you wanted to see her, even for a second. Did you forget? Did you ever ask yourself what I felt every time you talked to me about her?

Patrick: But that's not my fault. I didn't tell you to love me or to be the one to fix things between us. You made this big sacrifice.

Eleanor, her tears betraying her: Yes, me. Do you know why? Because I wanted to be close to you. I did this, telling myself every day maybe he'll feel me, maybe he'll love me half the love he has for her. Even after marriage, I prayed and cried every day, hoping a little love for me would grow in your heart.

Patrick: I didn't know you sacrificed so much for me.

Eleanor: Do you want to continue this sacrifice?

Patrick: Yes, continue.

Eleanor: After she left you, forced by her father to marry someone richer, you came to me, crying, asking what more you should have done, **Eleanor**? When you decided to marry me, I told myself maybe he forgot her and loves you. Maybe he felt your love for him and saw that you were the only one who stood by him. This was three years after her marriage, remember? After we got married, you insisted on having a daughter, not a son. When you knew it was a girl, on the day of her birth, you held her, left me, whispered something in her ear that only you and she heard. Then you decided to name her **Diana**. I didn't object when I saw your joy. You told me you loved the name and felt optimistic about it.

Eleanor, narrating through her tears, **Patrick** listening, remembering the day of **Diana**'s birth:

The nurse came out of the room: Congratulations, you have a beautiful baby girl.

Patrick was thrilled and entered the room.

Patrick: Congratulations to us, **Eleanor**.

Eleanor, joyfully: You achieved your dream today.

Patrick, happily: Yes, thank you.

Eleanor: I want to hold her for a bit.

Eleanor handed **Diana** to **Patrick**: Of course.

Patrick held **Diana** and left **Eleanor**.

Eleanor: Where are you going?!

Patrick didn't respond, moving away within the same room. He whispered in **Diana**'s ear: You've brightened my world, little one. Welcome. Do you know? I'll name you **Diana**. Do you want to know why? Because it's my favorite name. I want you to be like her, an angel. I promise I won't let anyone take you from me like they took her. You'll be the **Diana** I was deprived of. They didn't let me get enough of her, but I'll get enough of you.

He hugged her close, making **Diana** cry loudly.

Eleanor: What are you doing, **Patrick**?

Patrick, approaching **Eleanor**: Nothing, I was talking to **Diana**.

Eleanor, surprised: **Diana**!

Patrick: You don't mind naming her **Diana**, right? I love this name and feel optimistic about it.

Eleanor: Fine, as you wish. All I care about now is your happiness.

Back in the present, **Eleanor** continued:

Eleanor: You always scolded me whenever I argued with her or raised my voice. You favored her over **Ryan** and **Hana**. After **Diana**'s birth, you spent all your time with her, taking her out.

Patrick: Enough!!!

Patrick left the room, leaving **Eleanor** crying alone, and went outside the house.

During **Eleanor** and **Patrick**'s argument, **Ryan** and **Hana** were talking in **Hana**'s room.

Ryan: Come on, I'm listening. What happened?

Hana: Nothing. I found a better job, but it's a bit far from here.

Ryan: Is it abroad?

Hana: No, but far from here. So, I'll live alone.

Ryan: Do you want to leave us and go?

Hana: I don't want to stay with them.

Ryan: Why?

Hana: I'm tired of their arguments. They started again, can you hear them? Let's go to them.

Ryan: **Hana**, leave them.

Hana: But...

Ryan: This isn't new for them. Dad will leave Mom now and go. Then we'll go to her.

Five minutes later, they heard the house door close, knowing **Patrick** left. They went to **Eleanor**.

Hana: What happened, Mom? Why are you crying?

Hana, hugging her mother: Is it because of me? I'm sorry, I won't leave you.

Ryan stood outside the room, as if remembering something. He remembered every time his parents argued and his father left, leaving his mother crying alone. He remembered seeing his mother lost in thought with tears in her eyes or perhaps that night when he was twelve.

He heard his father talking to his friend about the love of his life, saying he still loved her and never forgot her. **Ryan** snapped out of his thoughts, left the house, and went to the place he always went to when the world felt too tight. Yes, the place he went to after arguing with **Matthew**. He walked, thinking about what to do. When he reached the place, he found **Matthew** sitting there.

Ryan, running towards **Matthew**: **Matthew**, what happened? Are you okay?

Matthew snapped out of his thoughts, finding **Ryan** beside him.

Matthew: What happened? When did you come here?

Ryan: What happened? Why did you come?

Matthew: Nothing. And you?

Ryan: Nothing.

Matthew: Do you want to stay silent?

Ryan: I'll leave.

Matthew: Go home?

Ryan: No, I'll leave the country again, and this time I won't come back.

Matthew: What? Are you crazy?

Ryan: Yes, I'm crazy. What am I doing here?

Matthew: And **Isabella**?

Ryan: She'll marry her boss.

Matthew: And **Diana**? Your family?

Ryan: My family! What family?

Matthew: **Ryan**, what happened?

Ryan: What happened with you? You didn't come here to relax.

Matthew: I argued with **Amelia** again.

Ryan: Because of me?

Matthew: Come on, tell me what happened.

Ryan: I didn't believe you, **Matthew**.

Matthew: Who called me?

Ryan: **Amelia**?

Matthew: No.

Ryan: Then who? Did **Ruby** call you?

Matthew: No, my mom.

Ryan: Are you joking? Who called you?

Matthew: I'm not joking. My mom called me.

Ryan, happily: What? Does she want to meet you?

Matthew: Yes.

Ryan: You should be very happy now, but why are you so sad?

Matthew: Because she called me because she wants money from me.

Ryan: What?

Matthew: Her son got sick, and she called to tell me he's very ill and needs a lot of money. She cried on the phone, asking me to do anything to get her the money.

Ryan: Why didn't the boy's father pay?

Matthew: He did, but he needs more money.

Ryan: **Matthew**, he's your brother. You'll help him, right?

Matthew, crying: I couldn't ask her why she didn't love me as much as she loved him. Aren't I her son too? She didn't cry for me. She left me, never called me since. She went, got married, had a son and a daughter with him. Today, she calls me, insisting I get her the money, saying he's my brother, and I should sacrifice for him.

Ryan, hugging him: But what fault is it of his? He's a child, **Matthew**.

Matthew: And what about my fault?

Ryan: Calm down, brother. How much money does she need?

Matthew: I won't help him, **Ryan**, I won't help him; but my heart aches. Why should I be harsh on a little child? He's my brother, even if I don't know his name or have never seen him. But he's still my brother. What should I do?

Ryan: What will we do? Have you forgotten that we are together, brother? We'll help him, of course. We won't let him bear the consequences of your mother's mistakes.

Matthew: But...

Ryan: Call her and find out how much money she needs. We'll arrange the amount, don't worry.

Matthew called his mother after trying to control his tears, to find out the details, how much money she needed, his brother's illness, and that he wanted to meet him first. After the conversation:

Ryan: Why did you want to meet him? Do you not believe her?

Matthew: I don't know; I want to see him first.

Ryan: How much money does she need?

Matthew: She said she'd ask the doctor about the operation cost.

Ryan: Don't worry, everything will be fine. I believe in that. Let's go from here, or do you want to stay?

Matthew: **Ryan**, you said she'd get married. How did you know?

Ryan: Did you know?

Matthew: Of course not, but how did you know?

Ryan: **Fiona** and I went to the restaurant I always went to with **Isabella**. I saw her with him, sitting together, and she told me he would be her fiancé. So, **Isabella** is no longer mine, brother.

Matthew: Will you really leave me and go? I have no one but you. Don't go.

Ryan: Then we'll go together.

Matthew: No, I can't leave **Amelia**.

Ryan: Then marry her.

Matthew: How? **Ryan**, I want you to help me complete my treatment.

Ryan: Really!

Matthew: Yes, and I also asked about **Victor** and **Diana** at the workplace you told me about.

Ryan: What did you find?

Matthew: They told me he's a good person, but I found out his full name.

Ryan: What's his name?

Matthew: Never mind his name now. When I saw his picture, it felt like I remembered him from somewhere, but I don't know where.

Ryan: Maybe you know him. Try to remember.

Matthew: Maybe we both know him.

Ryan: How?

Matthew: I don't know. Did **Diana** call you again?

Ryan: No, she didn't, and whenever I try to call her, her phone is off.

Matthew: What's this mystery?

Ryan: I don't know, but every time I remember **Hana** crying, I worry more about **Diana**.

Matthew: But your father won't leave her there, right? Your father loves **Diana** very much.

Ryan: That's what I don't understand. How did he let her go?

Matthew: Then ask him.

Ryan: I told you before, he doesn't tell me anything, and he doesn't want me to interfere.

Switching to **Amelia**'s house, where she and **Isabella** are talking:

Amelia: Why did you do that?

Isabella: I don't know, but I couldn't bear to see another girl next to him.

Amelia: **Isabella**, do you realize what you've done?

Isabella: Yes, I do. But what matters now is what he thinks.

Amelia: Who? **William**?

Isabella: **Ryan**.

Amelia: I'm really tired, **Isabella**. Think about **William**. What will he do? What situation did you put him in?

Isabella: He's very angry with me.

Amelia: I think he's right.

Isabella: Did you talk to **Matthew** today?

Amelia: Why?

Isabella: **Amelia**, what's happening between you and **Matthew**?

Amelia: That's what I want to know too. What's happening? Since **Ryan** returned, he's been preoccupied with him, leaving me.

Isabella: Maybe you are neglecting him, **Amelia**.

Amelia: What?

Isabella: **Amelia**, **Matthew** loves you, and you know that well. But he's afraid you'll leave him like his family did, so he always puts barriers between you.

Amelia: He never told me he wanted to marry me.

Isabella: Because he's afraid, and you never made him feel secure.

Amelia: What do you want me to do? Ask him to marry me?

Isabella: Of course not, but assure him you're always by his side.

Amelia: But I'm scared too.

Then **Isabella**'s phone rings.

Isabella: Wait.

Amelia: Who's calling you?

Isabella: It's **Hana**.

Amelia: Answer it then.

Isabella answered the phone.

Isabella: **Hana**, did something happen to **Ryan**?

Hana: No, but I need to meet you urgently.

Isabella: Why? What happened?

Hana: I need to meet you, **Isabella**, tomorrow.

Isabella: Okay, as you wish.

Hana: I'll send you the address. We'll meet before your work.

Isabella: Before work? At least after it.

Hana: No, **Isabella**, before work.

Isabella: Okay, **Hana**.

Isabella hung up with **Hana**.

Amelia: What happened?

Isabella: She wants to meet me!!

Amelia: Is it because of what happened?

Isabella: I don't know, but she said it's urgent.

Chapter Eight

The next day, in a park, **Hana** sat alone, waiting for **Isabella**, who arrived.

Isabella, hugging **Hana**: How are you?

Hana: Fine, and you?

Isabella: Fine.

Hana: Sit down, come on.

Isabella, sitting: Did something happen to him?

Hana, smiling: Does every conversation have to be about him?

Isabella: Of course not; but when you called and urgently asked to meet, I thought...

Hana, interrupting: Thought what?

Isabella: Nothing. **Hana**, are you okay?

Hana: No.

Isabella: What happened?

Hana: I'll summarize everything for you. But will you stand by me?

Isabella: Of course, **Hana**.

Hana: **Diana** got married and traveled.

Isabella: When? How?

Hana: She got married three months before **Ryan** returned.

Isabella: But I talked to you every day to check on him. Why didn't you tell me? And why are you sad about her marriage? I don't understand.

Hana: **Ryan** needs you by his side, **Isabella**.

Isabella: **Hana**, I don't understand anything. What's **Ryan**'s connection to her marriage? Why are you sad? And why didn't you tell me?

Hana: I think **Diana** married someone who isn't as good as he seems.

Isabella: Why? And how did your dad allow this? We all know how close he is to her. I don't understand anything.

Hana: I'll tell you everything that happened.

Hana explained everything.

Isabella: But how did your dad agree?

Hana: He doesn't know that **Victor** isn't a good person. **Diana** told me and made me promise not to tell anyone. But when she talked to me last time, I got very worried.

Isabella: Does **Ryan** know this?

Hana: No, I just told him she married someone not good. But I think he investigated and found nothing.

Isabella: Then tell him the whole truth and tell your dad too.

Hana: No, **Isabella**, I told you because I know you will help me.

Isabella: You mean my dad and brother?

Hana: Yes, please, **Isabella**, do everything to bring **Diana** back to us.

Isabella: But I think it's right to tell them, **Hana**.

Hana: Dad will get sick if he knows all this. And **Ryan**...

Isabella: What happened to him? I think he found someone to make up for all his past.

Hana: What do you mean?

Isabella: Didn't he tell you?

Hana: Tell me what?

Isabella: About her.

Hana: About whom?

Isabella: I saw him yesterday, sitting with a girl.

Hana: Who? **Ryan**, my brother?

Isabella: **Hana**, I'm not joking.

Hana: And I'm not joking. He didn't tell me anything since he returned. He only comes home at night or asks about **Diana**.

Isabella: I think he's with her.

Hana: Are you joking, **Isabella**? Do you still doubt his love for you!

Isabella: What love, **Hana**? What love? I still don't know why he left me, or why he came back. When I saw him, I saw him with her. Everything between us is over, **Hana**, everything is over this time.

Hana: How can everything be over?

Isabella's phone rang. She looked at it and then closed it.

Hana: Answer the phone. It's not a problem.

Isabella: It's not an important call.

Hana: Is it...?

Isabella: I'm not joking, **Hana**. Everything is over. Tell him she can stand by him; he doesn't need me. She's enough for him.

Hana: **Isabella**...

Isabella, standing: I'm very late for work.

She held **Hana**'s hand: Don't worry, **Diana** will come back safely. I'll tell my dad and brother everything today.

Hana, looking down: Will they agree to help the sister of someone who left their daughter and traveled without a reason?

Isabella: He doesn't deserve it, okay; but you're my sister, **Hana**. How can you doubt this? Dad and my brother treat you well, just like they treat me.

Hana: But **Diana**...

Isabella: This isn't the time.

Hana: But you know she didn't mean anything. I know you two didn't get along well.

Isabella: Not just her.

Hana, smiling and looking at her: You mean Dad too?

Isabella: **Hana**, I'm late for work. I'll go now. We'll talk later.

Isabella walked a few steps away from **Hana**.

Hana: **Isabella**.

Isabella turned to find **Hana** standing, moving towards her, and hugging her.

Hana: Thank you for everything.

Isabella, hugging her back: I won't forget you were always by my side despite everything.

Isabella stepped back: Come on, goodbye.

Switching to **Ryan** talking on the phone with **Fiona** while in **Matthew**'s car:

Fiona: How are you today?

Ryan: Fine, and you?

Fiona: I'm fine too. What are those sounds? Are you outside?

Ryan: Yes, with **Matthew**. We're going somewhere together.

Fiona: Give me the address, and I'll come too.

Ryan: No, **Fiona**, this is about **Matthew**.

Fiona: What happened?

Matthew stopped the car.

Matthew: This is the address you sent me.

Ryan: Okay.

Ryan continued with **Fiona**: **Fiona**, I have to go now. I'll talk to you later.

Fiona: Okay, goodbye.

They ended the call. **Ryan** looked at **Matthew**, who was staring ahead, lost in thought. **Ryan** patted his shoulder.

Ryan: Don't worry, I'm with you.

Matthew: But I'm worried.

Ryan: Why?

Matthew: This is the first time I'll see her after she left me. I'll see her husband and son.

Ryan: You'll see your brother, not just her son.

Matthew: You won't leave me alone, right?

Ryan: I'll come with you, don't worry.

They both got out of the car and went up to the fourth floor, specifically apartment 6b.

Matthew: Here, this is the apartment.

Ryan: Look at me. Don't worry, I'm with you. Everything will get better. Think about your brother.

Matthew took a deep breath and knocked on the door. His mother opened it. **Matthew** looked at her deeply and opened his arms to hug her, but she extended her hand to shake his instead. **Ryan** placed his hand behind **Matthew** to show he was with him this time, not with words but actions.

Matthew's mother, still extending her hand: **Matthew**, welcome.

Matthew closed his arms in sadness and extended his hand to shake hers.

Matthew: How are you, Mom?

Mother: Fine. Who is this?

Ryan lowered his hand from **Matthew**'s back and extended it to shake her hand: I'm **Ryan**, **Matthew**'s childhood friend. Don't you remember me?

Mother: No, I don't. Come inside.

Ryan looked at **Matthew** and saw him gazing at his mother with sorrow.

Ryan put his hand back on **Matthew**'s back: **Matthew**, let's go inside.

Matthew, snapping out of his thoughts: Okay.

Matthew's mother gestured to a specific room in the apartment: Come.

She opened the room to reveal a five-year-old boy.

Boy: Mom, where did you go?

Mother went to hug the child: I'm here, don't worry, **Liam**.

Matthew looked at them, tears streaming down his face, realizing he was deprived of such affection even when his mother was around. She never told him she was there for him. **Ryan** noticed and tightened his grip on **Matthew**'s shoulder.

Ryan whispered: **Matthew**, now's not the time.

Matthew, look at me.

Matthew left the room, followed by **Ryan**.

Matthew: I can't do this.

Ryan approached him, tightening his grip on both shoulders, whispering: What fault is it of this child's, **Matthew**? I won't let this hatred take away the love inside you.

111

Matthew: She never hugged me, not even once. I thought she'd hug me and cry when she saw me, but she didn't. She never told me she was there for me, but she told him she was there for him. Am I not her son too?

Ryan: **Matthew**, please, your brother needs you. Leave all this behind and wipe your tears.

Matthew's mother came out of the room: What happened?

Ryan stood in front of her, blocking her view of **Matthew** crying. He put his hand behind his back and handed him a tissue: Nothing, we'll be there now. Don't leave **Liam** alone.

Matthew took the tissue and wiped his tears.

Mother: Fine, I'll wait inside.

Ryan looked at **Matthew**: Come on.

They re-entered the room. **Ryan** placed a chair next to the bed where **Liam** sat.

Ryan: Sit here, **Matthew**.

Matthew sat, and **Ryan** stood beside him.

Liam: Who are these people, Mom?

Ryan: This is your brother, **Matthew**, and I'm **Ryan**.

Ryan extended **Matthew**'s hand to shake with **Liam**.

Liam, looking at his mother: How is he my brother, Mom?

Matthew, lowering his hand, looking at his mother: I want to talk to him a bit, if you don't mind.

Mother: Of course, it's your right.

Ryan put his hand on **Matthew**'s shoulder and leaned closer: I'll leave too and let you talk to him. If you need me, let me know. Remember, he's your little brother, don't take your anger out on him.

Matthew, smiling at **Ryan**: Don't worry.

Liam: Mom, don't leave me.

Mother: Don't worry, my son, he's your brother.

Liam: Don't leave me.

Matthew took out a small chocolate from his pocket.

Matthew: Look what I brought for you.

Ryan was surprised but left them and stepped outside, closing the door. Five minutes later, **Matthew**'s mother also stepped out. **Ryan** approached her.

Ryan: Do you mind if we talk for a bit?

Mother: But **Liam**...

Ryan: Leave them together, don't worry. **Matthew** won't hurt him.

Mother: I know, but **Liam** isn't good at talking to strangers.

Ryan: Strangers? This is his brother.

Mother: I know that, but does **Liam** know that?

Ryan: And whose fault is that?

Mother: What do you want?

Ryan: To talk for a bit.

They moved away from the room door and went to the living room, sitting down.

Ryan: Why?

Mother: I don't understand.

Ryan: Why do you do this to **Matthew**? Why do you hate him so much?

Mother: Does anyone hate their child?

Ryan: That's what I don't understand.

Mother: It's none of your business.

Ryan: It is my business because he's, my brother. You and his father hurt him a lot.

Mother: What do you want?

Ryan: I want to understand why you left him and his father.

Mother: I took care of him until he turned 18. I didn't leave him when he was young.

Ryan: Really! Does a mother leave her child when he turns 18? Is this a new law that's been applied without me knowing?

Mother: Are you mocking me?

Ryan: No, I can't. You're my brother's mother. Didn't you notice he wanted to hug you when he saw you today, but you deprived him of that too, hugging **Liam** in front of him? Are you telling me you left him when he turned 18 and really grew up? Fine, were you there for him throughout those 18 years? Did you hug him once like you hugged **Liam**?

Mother: Are you going to teach me how to treat my son?

Ryan: **Matthew** is your son too.

Mother: But he reminds me of him, the biggest mistake I made in my life.

Ryan: Reminds you of whom?

Mother: His father.

Ryan: And what fault is it of **Matthew**'s?

Mother, standing up: Please wait for **Matthew** outside. Keep your advice to yourself, not for others.

Ryan: I understand. But I'll tell you one thing: **Matthew** was mentally ill because of you and his father. I tried everything to fill the void you two caused, but there's nothing...

Ryan: "I understand, but I'll tell you one thing. **Matthew** was suffering from a psychological illness because of you and his father. I tried in every way to fill the void you caused, but nothing can compensate for the absence of parents in life. You have always thought only about yourself. Even when you spoke to him, it was for your own sake."

And **Ryan** leaves the house, waiting for **Matthew** by his car.

We then return to **Matthew** and **Liam** as they talk at the same time **Ryan** is speaking with **Matthew's** mother.

Matthew: "Do you like this type of chocolate?"

Liam: "Yes, thank you, but I cannot take it from you."

Matthew: "Why?"

Liam: "My mother told me not to take anything from a stranger."

Matthew: "But I'm not a stranger; I'm your brother."

Liam: "But my mother and father never told me I had a brother."

Matthew: "Well, let's make a deal. How about you let me be your big brother, and we'll play together, and I'll bring you everything you want?"

Liam: "Hmm, okay. I'll ask my mother about this, and if she agrees, I will too."

Matthew: "Okay."

Liam: "Do you not have a mother and father, so you call my mother your mother too?"

Matthew (sadly): "Do you mind if I hug you?"

Liam: "Wait, I'll ask my mother."

Matthew: "Look, **Liam**, you don't always have to take her opinion. Act as your heart tells you."

Liam: "And what does my heart say?"

Matthew: "I don't know; you tell me."

Liam: "It tells me that we will become friends."

Matthew (smiling): "So, do you mind if I hug you, my friend? Isn't a friend always supposed to hug his friend?"

Liam: "I don't know; I've never had friends before."

Matthew: "How come? Don't you have friends?"

Liam: "No, my mother didn't allow me to have friends in kindergarten."

Matthew: "Why?"

Liam: "I don't know. I don't know how to behave with my classmates. I'm always sitting alone, so I don't like going there."

Matthew (hugging him): "Don't worry; I'll be your friend, brother, and everything. I promise you'll be fine. I'll do everything to protect you."

Matthew steps back a little, stands up, and says: "I'll go now. Do you want anything?"

Liam: "Will you come back again?"

Matthew: "Do you want me to come always?"

Liam: "Yes."

Matthew (smiling): "Okay, I'll come. Just tell your mother you want to see me."

Matthew's mother opens the door angrily, looks at **Matthew**, and says: "Is this really your friend? Didn't his parents teach him how to talk to older people?"

Matthew (standing): "**Ryan**!! What happened?"

Liam: "Mom, I want **Matthew** to come always."

Matthew's mother looks in astonishment as **Matthew** approaches her and whispers: "I want to talk to you alone."

Matthew's mother: "Okay, **Liam**, I'll come now, don't worry."

Both of them leave the room. **Matthew** looks for **Ryan**, then turns to his mother and says: "Where is **Ryan**?"

His mother replies: "He's waiting for you outside."

Matthew: "Why? What happened?"

His mother: "Didn't his parents teach him how to deal with older people?"

Matthew: "Mom, **Ryan** is my brother. I won't let you treat him badly like you treat me. And also, why do you refuse to let **Liam** have friends?"

His mother: "**Liam** has a problem."

Matthew: "What is it?"

His mother: "He doesn't know how to deal with others."

Matthew: "How?"

His mother: "That's not our topic. What will you do now?"

Matthew: "He is my brother. I will do everything for him. And also, I'll come to sit with him if you don't mind."

His mother: "When will you bring the money?"

Matthew: "When do you want it, and how much do you need?"

His mother, opening the apartment door: "I'll tell you, of course. Thank you."

Matthew leaves the apartment, takes a few steps forward, then returns and says: "Where is my sister? I want to see her. What is her name?"

His mother: "But **Lara** is with her father outside. But wait, she is **Lara**, my daughter."

Matthew looks behind and sees a three-year-old girl holding her father's hand, walking towards her mother and hugging her.

Matthew kneels and stretches his hands to greet his sister.

Matthew: "**Lara**, how are you?"

Lara (to her mother): "Mom, who is this?"

Liam's and **Lara's** father: "Who is this?"

Matthew's mother: "This is **Matthew**; he came to check on **Liam**."

Liam's and **Lara's** father: "How are you, **Matthew**?"

Matthew does not reply but continues to look at **Lara**: "I am your brother, **Matthew**."

Lara: "I only have **Liam** as my brother."

Matthew's mother also kneels: "This is your brother too, **Lara**. What do we say when someone asks us how we are?"

Lara, extending her hand to shake his: "I'm fine. Look what my dad brought me?"

Matthew: "What did he bring you?"

She takes out two toys from the bag her father was carrying and says: "This is for me, and this is for my brother, **Liam**."

Matthew hugs her and says: "Go play with it inside and don't leave **Liam** alone."

Lara: "Will you come again?"

Matthew: "Of course."

Matthew takes out a chocolate bar from his pocket and gives it to **Lara**, just as he gave one to **Liam**.

Matthew: "I brought this for you."

Lara: "Thank you."

Liam's and **Lara's** father: "I'll leave you alone. We'll wait for you again, **Matthew**. This is your home, and these are your siblings, no doubt about it."

Matthew did not answer again and asks his mother.

Matthew: "Is **Lara**?"

His mother, smiling: "Yes, very social, unlike **Liam**. She talks to others and jokes with them."

Matthew, looking at his mother, wishing she would ask him to hug her: "Okay, I'll leave now."

His mother: "Okay. Goodbye."

Matthew goes down and looks back, seeing she has closed the door. He looks ahead sadly and goes to **Ryan**, who is standing by the car waiting for him. **Ryan** approaches him, putting his hands on **Matthew's** shoulders, and says:

Ryan: "Is everything okay?"

Matthew: "I saw **Lara**."

Ryan: "**Lara**!"

Matthew: "Yes, my sister."

Ryan: "Then why are you sad?"

Matthew: "Did you argue with my mother?"

Ryan: "No, did she say that to you?"

Matthew: "**Ryan**, tell me what happened?"

Ryan: "Nothing, brother. Did you talk to your siblings?"

Matthew: "I'll tell you what happened, but on the way. Come on."

Ryan: "**Matthew**, let me drive."

Matthew: "Okay."

They get in the car and **Ryan** drives it. **Matthew** tells him what happened.

Ryan: "I still don't understand, what is **Liam's** illness?"

Matthew: "I don't understand either. I don't even understand why he doesn't interact with others."

Ryan: "How can he not interact with others? He talked to you."

Matthew: "I don't know anything, **Ryan**. I don't know. Did you see how she treats **Liam** and **Lara** as if **Ruby** and I are not her children too?"

Ryan: "Don't be sad, brother, I'm with you. Where are we going now?"

Matthew: "I don't know."

Ryan: "Do you want to wander aimlessly?"

Matthew: "But we are already wandering aimlessly, **Ryan**."

Ryan: "I'll tell you something."

Matthew: "Go ahead."

Ryan: "I'm really proud of you."

Matthew, looking at him in astonishment: "Why?!"

Ryan: "Why not? You've overcome your sadness and hatred and treated your siblings well, brother."

Matthew: "Did you think I would make them pay the price?"

Ryan: "No, I knew there was goodness within you, and you would overcome your hatred."

Matthew: "But I loved them already."

Ryan: "Look, what else?"

Matthew: "I think her husband is good too."

Ryan: "I'll suggest something. Let's close this topic now. How about you call **Amelia** and you both go somewhere?"

Matthew: "**Amelia!** Where is she?"

They find **Matthew's** phone ringing. **Ryan** looks at the phone.

Ryan (laughing): "Is it her? What is this? Was she listening to us? Was she worried? Is she spying on us?"

Matthew: "For once, I want you to be quiet, brother, just once."

Ryan: "Okay, I'll be quiet."

Matthew answers her call.

Matthew: "Where are you?"

Ryan (laughing): "Why don't you talk to me with that voice too?"

Matthew gestures for him to be quiet.

Matthew: "Nothing, where are you?"

Amelia: "I called you to meet."

Matthew: "Really! Why?"

Amelia: "No reason. I thought a lot and found that we argue over things that don't concern us."

Matthew: "Did something fall on your head today?"

Amelia: "What!"

Matthew: "What happened, **Amelia**? Do you want us to argue today too?"

Amelia: "No, **Matthew**, I really want us to meet."

Matthew: "Okay, where are you?"

Amelia: "At work. We'll meet after your work and mine."

Matthew: "But I didn't go to work today."

Amelia: "Why? Are you okay?"

Matthew: "When we meet, I'll tell you. I'm coming to your workplace now. Tell **William** you want to leave early today."

Ryan gets angry when he hears **William's** name and speeds up the car. **Matthew** notices and says:

Matthew: "**Ryan**, what happened? Slow down."

Ryan speeds up even more, remembering the scene when he saw her with **William**, and she told him they were getting married.

Matthew: "**Ryan**, who am I talking to? Slow down. You'll cause an accident."

Ryan snaps out of his daydream and slows down, then stops the car.

Matthew: "**Amelia**, I'll talk to you again. Goodbye."

Amelia: "But..."

Matthew hangs up on her and focuses on **Ryan**.

Matthew: "What happened?"

Ryan: "Nothing, I just remembered something. Do you want me to take you to **Amelia**?"

Matthew understands what happened and says:

Matthew: "No, I'll take you home, and then I'll see **Amelia**."

Ryan, looking at him: "**Matthew**, I'm really fine. I'll take you to her, don't worry. I won't cause any trouble. Nothing is worth it anymore."

We go to **Isabella**, who is sitting in **William's** office.

William: "Why are you late today? Are you back to being late again?"

Isabella: "I was meeting a friend, and when you called me, I came quickly. I thought you wouldn't want to see my face today."

William: "Why?"

Isabella: "Because of what happened yesterday."

William: "What happened yesterday? I don't remember anything."

Isabella: "How?"

William: "**Isabella**, I said it happened, so nothing will change if I'm angry with you."

Isabella: "**William**, are you serious or are you..."

William: "I will ask you a question, **Isabella**, just once, and I want you to answer honestly."

Isabella: "Since when have I lied to you?"

William: "Okay, do you still love him? Look, if you say yes, nothing will happen; we will remain friends, and I will still listen to you and stay by your side, but only as a sister. If you say no, everything will change, and I will take a step towards you, but the important thing for me is that you tell the truth."

Isabella looks at the ground, then at **William**.

William: "I am listening."

At that moment, there is a knock on the door.

William: "Who is it?"

Amelia opens the door: "May I come in?"

William: "You always come at the right time, **Amelia**. Come in."

Amelia (smiling): "What happened? **Isabella**, aren't you working today?"

William: "What do you want, **Amelia**?"

Amelia: "I want to leave work early today."

William: "Why? Did something happen?"

Amelia: "Yes, I am meeting **Matthew**."

William: "Meet him after work."

Amelia: "What's this? **Isabella**, tell him to let me go."

Isabella: "What's it to do with me?"

Amelia: "Really! Okay, thank you both. I'll leave now."

William: "**Amelia**."

Amelia: "What? Do you want me to stay after work hours too?"

William: "No, go and meet him. I can't bear this anger around me, but this is the first and last time I'll allow this."

Amelia imitates him, "This is the first and last time I'll allow this." **Isabella** laughs, and **William** looks at her. **Amelia** leaves and they are alone again.

William: "Shall we return to our topic?"

Isabella: "Yes."

Isabella remembers the day he left her without any reason. She remembers crying for five years. She remembers waking up from nightmares where he left her. She remembers her family talking about how he left her and would never return. A conversation begins within her, between her heart and her mind.

Her heart answering her mind: "But he came back."

Her mind: "Did he come back for you?"

Her heart: "Why not?"

Her mind: "Did you forget the girl who was with him yesterday?"

Her heart: "But he will never forget me."

Her mind interrupts: "Wake up from this delusion. He left you, and when he came back, he had a girl by his side."

Her heart: "Will we really forget him?"

Her mind: "Will you cry for him again? Wasn't all this crying and sadness for him enough?"

Her heart: "I haven't forgotten."

Her mind: "Say that you have overcome his love."

Her heart: "But I don't want to lie to **William**."

Her mind: "You won't lie. He truly loves you and deserves you. He will make you love him."

Her heart: "But..."

William: "**Isabella**, where did you go, **Isabella**?"

Isabella snaps out of her thoughts and the conversation between her heart and mind.

Isabella: "What?"

William: "I was talking to you, and you were looking at me, but you weren't here. I told you to take your time to think."

Isabella (quickly): "No, I don't love him anymore, **William**. He is my past."

William: "**Isabella**, is this because of what happened yesterday?"

Isabella: "Of course not."

William: "Take your time to think, **Isabella**, and I will wait for your answer."

Isabella: "But I told you."

William: "Go back to work."

Isabella returns to her work.

We go back to **Matthew** and **Ryan** waiting for **Amelia** in the car.

Ryan looks at the factory, waiting to see her again.

Amelia arrives: "**Ryan**!"

Ryan: "Don't worry; I won't cause any trouble."

Amelia opens the back door and talks to **Matthew**: "I thought we would be alone, **Matthew**."

Matthew: "Get in."

Amelia: "**Matthew**, I am talking to you."

Matthew: "Drive the car, **Ryan**."

Amelia: "Where to?"

Ryan smiles and drives the car.

Amelia: "Where to, **Matthew**?"

Matthew: "Be quiet for a while. You'll make me change my mind."

Amelia: "What decision?"

Matthew (looking at **Ryan**): "Do all girls talk a lot, or just **Amelia**?"

Ryan smiles and stays quiet.

Amelia: "Okay, **Matthew**, I'll be quiet."

After half an hour...

Amelia: "What's this? You told me we would go out together. Why did you bring me home? I would have talked to my family on the phone and told them why we came."

Matthew: "Come on, let's get out."

Ryan stops the car.

Ryan: "I'll wait here."

Matthew: "No, you'll come with me. You are my only family."

Ryan: "But..."

Matthew (opening the door for him): "Come on, brother."

The three of them go up. **Amelia** knocks on the door. **Amelia's** mother opens the door.

Amelia: "Mom."

Amelia's mother: "Welcome, both of you. Come in."

Matthew: "How are you, son?"

Matthew: "I'm fine, and you?"

Amelia's mother: "I'm fine. **Ryan**, when did you come back?"

Ryan: "It hasn't been long since I returned. How are you?"

Amelia's mother: "I'm fine."

Amelia: "**Matthew** wanted to ask for your permission."

Matthew: "Where is **Amelia's** father, aunt?"

Amelia's mother: "He left work and is on his way home now. But why? Did something happen?"

Amelia: "Come on, ask for my mother's permission."

Matthew: "Wait until your father arrives."

Amelia's mother: "So, what would you like me to offer you?"

Matthew and **Ryan**: "Nothing, thank you."

Amelia: "I'll get them something to drink, mom."

After a short while, **Amelia's** father arrives.

Amelia's father: "How are you, young men?"

Matthew and **Ryan**: "Fine."

Matthew: "Uncle, I wanted to talk to you about something important."

Amelia's father: "Did something happen?"

Matthew (looking at the ground and rubbing his hands): "No, but I..."

Ryan places his hand on **Matthew's** back to remind him he's there. **Matthew** looks at **Ryan** for encouragement and then looks at **Amelia's father**.

Matthew: "I came to ask for **Amelia's** hand in marriage, uncle. Do you accept?"

Amelia stands, her eyes filled with tears of joy: "What? Are you joking? What did you say?"

Matthew continues: "**Ryan** is my family, so I brought him with me. You know that my parents left me alone years ago, and since then, I've been relying on myself for everything."

Chapter Nine

Amelia, still in disbelief: "Mom, Dad."

Amelia's father: "Look, son, we know that you and **Amelia** love each other, but..."

Ryan: "But what, uncle? You won't find someone who loves **Amelia** as much as he does."

Amelia's father: "And his family?"

Amelia: "Dad."

Amelia's mother: "**Amelia**, go inside."

Amelia: "What, mom?"

Amelia's father looks at **Amelia**, signaling her to go to her room. **Amelia** goes to her room sadly. She had been waiting for this day for a long time, and when it came, her father would refuse. **Matthew** had been afraid of this moment for a long time, which is why he hesitated to take this step.

Ryan: "I don't understand."

Amelia's father: "I won't let my daughter be with someone whose family left him, and I don't even know why."

Matthew: "I don't understand why you reject me. Do I have to pay for them leaving me? Should I have lied to you for you to agree?"

Amelia's father: "No, it's brave of you, and I know you're a good person, but..."

Ryan: "But what? As long as you know he's a good person, what does his family matter?"

Amelia's father: "Look, **Matthew**, none of us chooses our family, but your father isn't a good man."

Matthew: "But he left me. I don't know anything about him."

Amelia's father: "But I know everything about him."

Matthew: "What? What do you know about him to reject me?"

Ryan looks at **Amelia's father** and stays silent.

Matthew: "Look, uncle, I love **Amelia**. Not from today or yesterday, but since childhood. Yes, my parents left me, but I promise I won't leave her. And you wouldn't allow her to leave me either. That's why I came to ask you to let her be by my side."

Amelia's father looks at his wife: "Let me think about it."

Matthew: "Will you agree?"

Ryan: "Let's go, **Matthew**."

Matthew and **Ryan** leave the house.

Matthew (talking to **Ryan**): "I told you. Do you see now why I always refused to propose to her?"

Ryan: "Will you run away for the rest of your life? Will you leave the girl you love for a sin you didn't commit?"

Matthew: "I didn't commit it, true, but my parents did. They left me and didn't stop. I know **Amelia's** father is worried about her, not because of me but because of my father. I wish I hadn't listened to your advice. I wish I hadn't proposed to her."

Ryan: "Did you want to stay with her like this without marriage?"

Matthew (getting into his car): "I want to be alone."

Ryan: "**Matthew**, it's not the time."

Matthew drives away.

Ryan hails a taxi and goes home. We return to **Matthew**.

Matthew's inner thoughts: "Will I pay for a sin that's not mine? Will I spend the rest of my life paying the price for the past? They never let me forget what happened for a moment. Every time I tried to forget, something reminded me again. I tried to stay alive without the past haunting me, but to no avail. I've seen a lot in my years. I tried to escape by sleeping, but everything I ran from came to me in my dreams. So, I decided to run away in another way, to leave everything and go forever.

But I realized that's not the solution. The pain will subside, of course, but am I ready to die now? No, I'm not ready. I'm scared. So, I tried to escape in another way, to leave the country, to leave all the places, images, and people who hurt me. But the problem isn't in the country; it's in my mind that always remembers them. Finally, I decided to face it, not run away. But this solution pains me greatly. Every time I face what hurts me, I find myself bleeding again. I find myself crying alone in my room. I have no more tears to cry and no one to listen to me. Everyone I defended and fought for fought against me. What will I do now?"

We return to **Amelia**, who is coming out of her room, crying heavily and talking to her father.

Amelia: "Why, Dad?"

He doesn't answer her.

Amelia: "It's not his fault. What does he have to do with his father? Are you saying his father isn't good? He doesn't know anything about him, doesn't know anything you know."

Amelia's father: "But he's still his father."

Amelia: "He's not his father. A father doesn't leave his son and go."

Amelia's father: "What do you want? Do you really want to marry him?"

Amelia: "Why not? I love him, Dad. Were you really cruelling to him instead of telling him we will be his new family?"

Amelia's father: "Will we become a family to someone whose parents didn't take care of him?"

Amelia: "But you never taught me this cruelty."

Amelia goes to her room to get her phone and leaves the house.

Amelia's mother: "**Amelia**, where are you going?"

Amelia's father: "Let her go."

Amelia's mother: "Why did you do this? You know **Matthew** well."

Amelia's father: "**Amelia** is my only daughter. Do you want me to sacrifice her?"

Amelia's mother: "No, but **Matthew** is a good person and really loves her. Don't tell me about his father. You know he knows nothing about his father."

Amelia's father: "What will happen if his father shows up in his life again?"

Amelia's mother: "I don't know, but he won't come back after all these years."

Amelia's father: "Everyone grows up to be like their parents, no matter how far they try to distance themselves or become different."

We then switch to **Amelia** talking on the phone with **Isabella**.

Amelia: "Where are you?"

Isabella: "I just finished work, and I'm going out with **William**, but are you okay?"

Amelia: "No, I want to talk."

Isabella: "What happened?"

Amelia: "I'll tell you when we meet."

Isabella: "Okay, **William** and I are going to a place to sit. Do you want to come, or would you rather meet at my house?"

Amelia: "No, I'll come with you."

Isabella: "I'll send you the address."

Amelia: "Okay."

They hang up.

William (while driving): "What happened?"

Isabella: "I don't know, she'll tell me when she gets here."

Then she looks at him and says: "You won't be upset, right?"

William: "Of course not. Did you fight with him?"

Isabella: "I don't know, we'll understand soon."

An hour later, **William** and **Isabella** are sitting, waiting for **Amelia**.

Isabella: "Why is she so late?"

William: "Here she comes."

Amelia looks at **William** and is hugged by **Isabella**.

Isabella: "What happened, **Amelia**?"

The three sit down.

Amelia: "He proposed to me."

Isabella (excitedly): "Really! I knew he would take this step. So, why are you so sad?"

Amelia: "My father didn't agree."

Isabella: "Why?"

Amelia (closing her eyes): "Because of **Matthew's** family."

Isabella: "I don't understand. Your parents know **Matthew** well. What does his family have to do with this? They know they left him."

Amelia: "Because of **Matthew's** father."

Isabella: "I don't understand."

William: "Do you want me to leave and give you two some privacy?"

Amelia: "No, **William**, you're not a stranger."

Isabella: "What happened with his father, **Amelia**?"

Amelia (crying): "My father knows everything about him."

Isabella: "So, what's the problem?"

Amelia: "You know my father and **Matthew's** father were friends from the beginning."

Isabella: "Yes, **Amelia**, **Matthew's** father wasn't very stable from a young age. When he left his son and went away, he met new people who weren't good, and they made him like them over time."

Isabella: "I don't understand."

Amelia: "**Isabella**, his money isn't clean. That's all I'll say."

Isabella: "Does **Matthew** know this?"

Amelia: "No, my father told me this at the time, and I didn't tell **Matthew**. It would have destroyed him."

William: "Do you want my opinion?"

Amelia: "Of course."

William: "Your father is right."

Amelia: "No, **Matthew** doesn't know anything about his father. **Matthew** works and spends on himself with his own money. **Matthew** is completely different from him."

William: "But he's still his father, **Amelia**, no matter what. Maybe he'll go back to him."

Isabella: "But he hasn't returned all these years. Will he return now?"

William: "Why not?"

Isabella: "No, **Amelia**, listen to me. Talk to your father again, or wait and talk to **Matthew** first. I think he's shattered now; you need to stand by him."

Amelia: "But he didn't answer his phone, and I don't know where he is."

Isabella (looking at the ground): "Did you call **Ryan**?"

Amelia: "Yes, but he told me that **Matthew** went alone."

Isabella (thinking): "Where would he go?"

Amelia: "To his house!"

Isabella: "Or to..."

Amelia: "Do you think so?"

Isabella: "Of course, whenever either of them is in trouble, they go there. Let's go."

William: "I'll drive you."

Isabella: "You're coming with us."

William: "I'll drop you off and go back home."

Isabella: "No, **William**, you'll stay with us. **Matthew** isn't a stranger."

William: "He's not a stranger, but he's still **Ryan's** friend. He won't be happy to see me with you, and this is about **Matthew** and **Amelia**, not me."

Isabella: "Come on, **William**."

The three go to the place where either of them goes when they're in trouble and find **Matthew** sitting alone.

William: "**Isabella**, I don't agree with you."

Isabella: "**Amelia**, talk to him alone."

Amelia gets out of the car.

Amelia: "**Matthew**."

Matthew hears her voice but doesn't turn around.

Amelia: "**Matthew**."

She approaches him, puts her hand on his shoulder, and sits next to him.

Amelia: "We'll solve everything, don't worry. I'm with you; I won't leave you."

Matthew: "But he's right."

Amelia: "What? Will you give up on me that easily?"

Matthew: "I didn't give up on anyone, but everyone I loved gave up on me."

Amelia: "I'm not like them."

Matthew: "Like who? My family! My family that should have been with me and never left me."

Amelia: "What's new, **Matthew**?"

Matthew: "New! There's nothing new, but the past always haunts me."

Ryan arrives at this moment and sees a car. He approaches it to find **Isabella** and **William** sitting inside, looking at **Amelia** and **Matthew**. **Ryan** puts his hands on the car window next to **William**.

Ryan (looking at her): "Why did you come?"

William looks at **Isabella** and stays silent.

Isabella: "What's it to you?"

Ryan: "What's it to me! Do you want **Matthew**'s fate to be like mine?"

Isabella: "No, because he loves her, unlike you."

Ryan: "Yes, you're right. That's why fate compensated you with someone who loves you, right, **William**?"

William: "What do you want?"

Ryan: "Nothing. Take her away and leave. I will handle **Amelia** and **Matthew**'s situation."

Isabella: "How will you handle it? Will you encourage him to travel and leave her like you did?"

Ryan: "Take her and leave. When is your engagement so I can attend?"

Isabella gets out of the car and heads towards **Amelia** and **Matthew**. **Ryan** follows her, and **William** looks at them.

Isabella: "**Amelia**."

Matthew stands up and looks at them.

Matthew: "**Isabella**!"

Isabella: "What will you do, **Matthew**?"

Ryan: "**Isabella** thinks you'll travel and leave **Amelia**."

Amelia: "What?"

Isabella (looking at **Ryan**): "What do you want from me? Isn't what happened in the past enough? Leave me alone!"

Ryan: "What do you want? You came here with him. This place was only known by you, me, **Matthew**, and **Amelia**."

Isabella: "What's the problem?"

Ryan: "I'm tired of this."

Isabella: "Tell yourself, **Ryan**, enough. Leave me alone. Didn't she compensate you for me?"

Ryan: "Be sure of that, just like he compensated you for me."

Matthew and **Amelia**: "Enough, enough."

Amelia: "We came to find a solution, not for you two to fight."

Amelia: "I'll go and ask **William** to join us, and we can think about what to do."

Ryan: "**Amelia**, are you joking?"

Amelia: "No."

Ryan approaches **Matthew**: "Will you fight with me as before, or will I fight alone?"

Matthew: "Calm down, **Ryan**."

They all sit down, with **Amelia** beside **Matthew**, **Ryan** next to **Matthew**, and **Isabella** sitting between **William** and **Ryan**.

Amelia: "What will we do now?"

William: "What do you think about ordering food first?"

Ryan (sarcastically): "Yes, that's the solution, folks."

William: "I mean we can't think clearly when we're hungry."

Ryan: "**Matthew**, whenever you're in trouble, talk to **William** for a solution."

Isabella: "Yes, I'm very hungry."

Ryan: "Then let's order food."

Matthew (laughing): "What happened, brother? We were about to find a solution."

Ryan: "Let's eat first, then we'll find one."

Amelia: "Then let's go to a restaurant and eat."

Matthew: "Okay, who will ride with whom?"

Amelia: "I'll ride in your car, and **Isabella** with **William**. **Ryan**, how did you come?"

William: "It's not a problem. He can ride with me and **Isabella**."

Ryan: "I'll ride with **Matthew**. On the way, I'll call **Fiona** to join us."

Isabella: "Yes, yes, I wanted to meet her."

Ryan: "Then I'll make your wish come true."

William stands up and holds **Isabella**'s hand. **Ryan** looks at them angrily, and **Matthew** approaches him.

Matthew: "Calm down, close your eyes."

Ryan closes his eyes to calm down. **Isabella** looks at **Ryan** and then at **William**, holding his hands. They both get into the cars. **Ryan** calls **Fiona** to come, and they all sit at the restaurant.

Fiona: "Tell me a little about yourself, **Isabella**. I know a lot about you, but I'd rather hear from you."

Isabella: "Tell you what?"

Fiona: "Anything about you."

William: "Let me tell you about her."

Ryan: "Please, go ahead."

William: "**Isabella** is excellent at her job. I see a bright future for her, unlike others. She's gentle, smart, and pure, acting naturally."

Ryan looks at him angrily, trying to calm down and not show his jealousy. He closes his eyes, and both **Matthew** and **Amelia** laugh.

Ryan (opening his eyes again): "You're really lucky to make a girl like **Isabella** fall in love with you."

Isabella looks at **William** silently. **William** responds calmly while eating.

William: "I understand you well, **Ryan**. Anyone in your position would do this, but it's not a problem. What's important is the present and the future, not the past. We all have a past and love story, but they failed."

Matthew looks at **Ryan**, knowing he will get angrier now.

Amelia: "What do you think of the food? It's delicious, isn't it?"

Isabella (leaning towards **William**, speaking softly): "What are you doing?"

William: "Nothing."

Fiona: "I agree with you, **William**. We were all living in an illusion called love, but it became the past. So, we should focus on the present."

Matthew: "I don't agree with you both. People meet many others, but there's only one person who will enter your life and take a place no one else can. Maybe you won't be together, but you'll never forget them as long as you live."

Isabella: "Why, **Matthew**? Should someone stay stuck in a failed past relationship? Maybe you'll meet someone who makes you think everything that happened in your life was just a prelude to them. One right person makes you forget all the past pain and failure. Perhaps what you went through was necessary to appreciate the right person."

Ryan: "So, **William** is very happy now because he's the right person."

William laughs and continues eating, provoking **Ryan** more.

Fiona: "I agree with you."

She looks at **Ryan** and says: "I didn't feel alive until I met you."

Isabella: "I think you should take it slow until, you're sure."

Fiona: "Why? What **Ryan** and I went through wasn't small, right, **Ryan**?"

Ryan (smiling at her): "Yes."

Amelia (leaning towards **Matthew**, speaking softly): "I think this meal's end will be catastrophic."

Matthew smiles at her and then says to everyone: "I think we forgot the main topic, folks."

Fiona: "But it's not a problem, **Matthew**. Convince her family to agree. As long as you two love each other, there's no issue."

Isabella: "You speak rationally, **Fiona**. I suppose that's why **Ryan** loves you because he loves rational people who talk like you. But unfortunately, he'll leave you without any reason, leaving you to wonder why he left."

Ryan: "Without reason."

Fiona: "Don't worry, **Isabella**. It depends on the girl he's with. Maybe a man gets bored of the girl he's with, so he leaves her."

Isabella: "What do you mean?"

William: "If he did that, it would be the biggest mistake of his life because someone who loves **Isabella** will never get bored of her. Also, someone in love won't get bored, **Fiona**, unless it was a false love."

Amelia: "Guys, calm down a bit. This isn't a war."

Ryan: "Maybe the one in front of me was too stupid."

Isabella: "Stupid!"

Ryan: "Yes, thinking someone left without a reason is stupid."

Isabella: "Then what's the reason?"

At this moment, **Ryan's** phone rings, and he sees it's his mother calling.

Ryan: "Mom."

Eleanor: "**Ryan**, where are you?"

Ryan: "Out. What happened, Mom?"

Eleanor: "**Diana**."

Ryan (standing up): "What about her?"

Chapter Ten

Eleanor (crying): "**Diana** has returned, **Ryan**."

Ryan: "Really! So why are you crying now?"

Eleanor: "You need to come."

Ryan ends the call.

Fiona: "What happened?"

Ryan: "**Diana** has returned."

Matthew: "Returned how? Did he come back with her?"

Ryan: "I don't know. I have to go now."

Matthew: "Wait for me; I'll come with you."

Fiona: "Me too."

Amelia, **Isabella**, and **William** remain seated.

Isabella: "So what you told me, **Hannah**, was wrong."

Amelia: "What?"

Isabella (to **William**): "What happened to you?"

William: "What happened to me!"

Isabella: "**William**, this is the first time I see you talk like this and with such provocation."

William: "What about him? Was he speaking correctly?"

Isabella: "Okay, did you see how **Fiona** deals with him?"

William: "I think you need to wake up from this delusion, **Isabella**."

Isabella: "**William**!!"

Amelia: "If you're done eating, let's go."

We move to **Ryan**, **Matthew**, and **Fiona** when they arrived at **Ryan's** house. **Ryan** knocks on the door, and **Hannah** opens it.

Ryan: "Where's **Diana**?"

Hannah: "Inside."

Ryan moves, but **Hannah** holds him back and says:

Hannah: "Calm down first, then see her."

Ryan: "**Hannah**, is she okay?"

Hannah: "**Ryan**, calm down, please."

Matthew: "Don't worry, I'm with him."

Everyone enters and sees **Diana** sitting, but her face shows signs of beating and bruises.

Ryan: "**Diana**, what is this?"

Diana goes to him and hugs him. **Ryan** and **Diana** cry. **Eleanor** sits crying, while **Patrick** sits silently without any reaction. **Ryan** holds **Diana**'s arms and finds her in pain.

Ryan: "What? What happened to you?"

Hannah: "**Ryan**."

Hannah gently holds **Diana**'s hand and makes her sit down again. **Fiona** talks to **Matthew** in a low voice.

Fiona: "**Matthew**, I'm leaving."

Matthew: "Why?"

Fiona: "I think it's a family matter; it's not my place to stay."

Matthew: "Okay, I'll stay here."

Fiona: "Okay."

Fiona leaves.

Ryan: "What happened, sister? How did you come back? Where is he, and what happened to you?"

Diana: "I ran away from him and returned."

Ryan: "Did he do this to you?"

Diana cries, and **Hannah** stands up.

Hannah: "**Ryan**, I need you for a minute, and you too, **Matthew**."

The three of them move away from the others.

Matthew: "What happened to her?"

Hannah: "I told you before, **Ryan**, he's not a good person. I knew all this."

Ryan: "Knew what?"

Hannah: "**Ryan**, she ran away from him, but she's still scared of him."

Matthew: "But we'll find him and hold him accountable for this, don't worry."

Hannah: "Hold him accountable? Do you think he's someone you can fight with?"

Matthew: "So we'll leave him like this?"

Ryan: "We have to find him first, then think about what to do next. But I don't even have any information about him."

Matthew: "**Hannah**, what do you think about talking to her?"

Hannah: "No, no, she's scared now."

Ryan: "How did Dad agree to this person?"

Hannah: "**Ryan**, Dad didn't know."

Ryan: "But he's sitting there, saying nothing."

Matthew: "What do you mean? Did he know and allow this, **Ryan**?"

Hannah: "I'll try to talk to her when she calms down. **Ryan**, try to calm down so we can solve this problem."

Ryan: "I'll go get some fresh air."

Matthew and **Ryan** go out together.

Ryan: "I can't handle all this. If I talk to my dad now, he'll say I left my siblings."

Matthew: "**Ryan**, you need to calm down so we can think."

Ryan: "Think about what? Where's **Fiona**?"

Matthew: "She left."

Ryan: "When?"

Matthew: "When she saw **Diana** in that condition, she left."

Ryan: "Really! I didn't see her."

Matthew: "I'm going now. If you need anything, call me."

Ryan: "Okay, brother."

Matthew: "But wait, what will you do now to calm down?"

Ryan: "I'll do what I always did when I was away."

Matthew: "You mean you'll write on paper."

Ryan: "Yes, go ahead."

Ryan goes back to his house.

Ryan: "Mom, where's **Diana**?"

Eleanor: "In her room, resting."

Ryan goes to **Diana** and **Hannah**'s room and gently opens the door. He finds **Diana** asleep and **Hannah** sitting beside her, watching her sleep. He closes the door and goes to his room, grabs a piece of paper, places it in front of him, picks up his pen, and begins to write, as it's the only way he can express his inner feelings.

(I expected that once I returned, everything would be as it was, but it wasn't. What happened was that I found myself more lost in my own country. I returned to my loved ones, but I found them changed; they were not the same as when I left them. Perhaps my only problem during my time away was my absence itself.

Being away from my loved ones, although I always checked on them, now I am with them but feel abandoned. Maybe the distance wasn't in the miles but in the hearts. When I was in a distant country, they were always with me, and I with them. Now, we are in the same country, but our hearts have drifted apart.

Does anyone want to leave and abandon their loved ones? Ah, the pain of exile I endured for many years just to protect my loved ones. I threw myself into the fire to let them be in bliss, and now they accuse me of being in bliss and leaving them in the fires of separation and longing.)

At that moment, **Ryan** hears a girl's loud scream. He leaves everything and rushes out to find the sound coming from his siblings' room. He finds **Eleanor** and **Patrick** standing in front of the room.

Hannah: "**Diana**, **Diana**, wake up, come on."

Hannah: "**Diana**, it's just a nightmare, wake up."

Ryan approaches **Diana**: "**Diana**, wake up."

Diana wakes up in panic, saying: "No, no, I didn't do anything."

Ryan: "Calm down, you're safe."

Hannah: "It was just a nightmare, sister, don't worry."

Eleanor: "**Diana**, are you okay?"

They find **Diana** trembling with fear. **Eleanor** sits beside her, hugs her, and tries not to cry to calm her down. **Ryan** looks at his father standing silently.

Ryan (approaching him): "Dad, let's stand on the balcony."

They both go together.

Ryan: "Dad, are you okay?"

Patrick: "Yes."

Ryan: "Dad."

Patrick: "This is the second time I've lost **Diana**."

Ryan: "So why did you agree to him, dad?"

Patrick: "I didn't agree to him, but what could I do? I found her deeply in love with him, **Ryan**. I didn't expect all this to happen. I feel helpless for the third time."

Ryan: "For the third time?"

Patrick: "I couldn't protect either of them, whether it was older **Diana** or younger **Diana**."

Ryan: "Dad, are you standing in front of me to tell me about your old love?"

Patrick: "You're right. I'll tell you a secret you won't know until you become a father."

Ryan: "What is it, dad?"

Patrick: "True helplessness is feeling you can't prevent harm from reaching your children. You'll feel like a bird with broken wings."

Ryan: "Dad."

Patrick: "I couldn't protect her. I couldn't be a good father to you. Maybe I should have insisted on rejecting him. She would have cried for a day or two, no more. But now, she'll cry for the rest of her life. I didn't want to be like him and let you live as you wished. You traveled, she married who she loved. I didn't want you to come to me one day and ask why I rejected him. I didn't want to tie her unhappiness to my rejection of him. And when I found out I failed, I wanted to use the same method

Diana's father, the father of my old love, as you say, used to care for **Hannah**. I found myself failing too. So, what do I do now?"

Ryan: "We'll find him, make him divorce her, and try to get her to tell us in detail what happened."

Patrick: "Can you listen to what happened?"

Ryan: "No. Why did you always treat me harshly, dad?"

Patrick: "I wanted you to become a strong person. When you left, I was very angry with you, but I wished I were like you when I was your age."

Ryan: "How? Did you want to travel?"

Patrick: "I wanted to escape from myself."

Ryan: "But I found that running away wasn't a solution, so I returned."

Patrick: "**Ryan**, don't leave **Isabella**. Do everything to have her back. Believe me, son, if you leave her, she'll always stay inside you, and you won't get rid of her."

Ryan: "If only everything were that simple, dad."

Patrick: "What happened?"

Ryan: "I think I came back to her too late. But thank you for the advice. I think it's the first time we've talked this openly."

Patrick: "You will always be my little son, no matter what happens."

Ryan: "Do you still love her, dad? Didn't mom succeed in making you love her?"

Patrick: "Who told you I didn't love your mom? I love her very much because she's the mother of my children and the person who endured me the most. But I won't lie; no one could ever take **Diana's** place. Life goes on, son, but it continues with something missing, something that can never be replaced."

Ryan: "Does that mean I'll never forget her?"

Patrick: "It wouldn't be love if you forgot it, son. In this life, you'll see everything you loved in someone else's hands. Each of us has experienced the feeling of being deprived of something or someone they love dearly at least once in their life. When you go through this feeling, you'll find yourself no longer wishing for anything, turning into a person with numb feelings."

Ryan: "If only we never grew up, dad, if only we stayed children, our only goal being to play."

At this moment, **Eleanor** comes and says:

Eleanor: "What are you talking about?"

Ryan: "Is **Diana,** okay?"

Eleanor: "Yes, she's calmed down and gone back to sleep. I left **Hannah** with her."

Ryan: "Do we need to take her to a doctor?"

Eleanor: "**Patrick**, we need to make him divorce her."

Ryan: "Don't worry, Mom. I'll take care of it."

Patrick: "I trust you."

Ryan: "Where is he? What's his name? Anything about him?"

Eleanor: "But what if he tries to come and harm her?"

Ryan: "She was alone there, but here he can't harm her. We're with her."

Patrick: "**Ryan** is right."

We switch to **Isabella**, who has gone to her family's villa and enters her parents' room.

Isabella: "Mom."

Sophia: "When did you come?"

Isabella: "Just now. I need to tell you something."

Sophia: "What?"

Isabella: "There's someone who wants to meet you and Dad."

Sophia (smiling): "Does that mean?"

Isabella: "Mom, he just wants to meet my family. Don't make it a big deal."

Sophia: "I was afraid you'd go back to **Ryan** when he returned."

Isabella: "There's a girl in his life now, Mom. He loves someone else."

Sophia: "Are you upset?"

Isabella: "No, that was the past. It's time to write a new story with a new hero."

Sophia: "I wish you happiness always, my daughter."

Isabella: "Alright, when will you meet **William**?"

Sophia: "**William**! Is he the son of the factory owner where you work?"

Isabella: "Yes, he's now heading the work instead of his father."

Sophia: "I'll tell your father."

Isabella: "How about tomorrow?"

Sophia: "Tomorrow!"

Isabella: "Yes, tomorrow after work, and we all have dinner here."

Quentin (**Isabella**'s father) enters the room.

Quentin: "May I come in?"

Sophia: "**Isabella** has good news for you."

Isabella: "Mom, don't make it a big deal."

Quentin (sitting down): "What is it? Tell me. Or first, tell me what you did at work today?"

Isabella: "Dad, there's someone who wants to meet you, and I think we should invite him for dinner tomorrow after work. What do you think?"

Quentin: "Wait, what happened?"

Isabella: "What happened?"

Quentin: "Why the rush? Who is he? Why tomorrow? Why does he want to meet us?"

Isabella: "Mom will tell you everything. I'll invite him for tomorrow, and now I'll go to my room to rest a bit. Tell **Gabriel** too."

Quentin: "I don't understand anything."

Sophia: "I'll tell you."

Isabella goes to her room and sends two messages, one to **Hannah** and the other to **William**.

Message to **Hannah**: (**Hannah**, is everything alright? What happened to **Diana**?) Message to **William**: (I told my family you will come tomorrow after work. I'll be waiting for you.)

Then she leaves her phone and stands in front of the mirror, speaking to herself as if two people are talking.

Her mind: "You will succeed in this. Don't worry. **William** is a good person and deserves you."

Her heart: "But what about him?"

Her mind: "He loves her."

Her heart: "You know he won't love another girl besides you."

Her mind: "That's not true. This story is over."

Her heart: "At least make sure he's alright."

Her mind: "What's it to me?"

Her heart: "Why have you become so harsh?"

Her mind: "I learned this harshness from him. This story is over. From tomorrow, a new story begins with a new hero. The conversation ends here."

Dinner time comes, and everyone sits down.

Quentin: "Tell us about yourself, **William**."

William: "Okay, my name is **William**, I am 30 years old, and I took over the work after my father's illness. I now live with my father, and I have one brother, **Jude**, who is two years older than me."

Gabriel: "Do you like to travel?"

Isabella: "What do you mean, **Gabriel**?"

Gabriel: "Nothing."

William: "Don't worry."

Everyone finishes their meal.

Quentin: "**Gabriel**, take **William** and sit in the garden until I come."

Isabella and **Sophia** bring something for **William** to drink.

Gabriel: "Come on, **William**."

They go and sit in the garden.

William: "You can speak now as you wish."

Gabriel: "You're very smart."

William: "You could say I'm good at understanding people."

Gabriel: "I'll tell you something. I don't know if **Isabella** told you or not."

William: "Do you mean about her previous engagement? Yes, I know, and I've met **Ryan** several times."

Gabriel: "Really!"

William: "Yes."

Gabriel: "**Isabella** is my only sister. I'm afraid what happened to her will happen again. Well, you met **Ryan**, and **Isabella** told you about him, but I don't think she told you everything."

Gabriel continues: "**Isabella** was shattered because of him, **William**. Even saying she was shattered is an understatement. None of us could save her or ease her pain. For five years, she waited for him. She loved him with every part of her, **William**."

William: "**Gabriel**, I know all of this."

Gabriel: "No, you don't know. Imagine seeing your only sister broken, crying all day because of someone. She doesn't want to do anything. Believe me, no matter what I tell you, I can't explain it. My mom, dad, and I are happy that she got over this love and tried to give someone else a chance because we were trying to help her. I don't want the same thing to happen again. She can't bear this pain again. I was very angry when I found out he came back. I thought she'd go to him as if he didn't steal five years from her, as if he didn't leave her crying alone. But I was really surprised by what happened. I don't want you to be angry with me, but **Ryan** was like a brother to me, and he did this to my sister. So, what will happen from someone I don't know anything about?"

William: "**Gabriel**, I..."

Gabriel: "If you want to leave, leave now. If you stay, never leave. That's all I want to tell you, not just me but my mom and dad too."

William: "Don't worry about her."

Sophia: "I brought you some juice."

Isabella: "What are you two talking about?"

William: "Nothing."

The day ends, and **William** returns home. After two weeks, we return to **Ryan** and his family.

Ryan (calmly): "We've left you for two weeks to rest, and the psychologist told us you could tell us. So, **Diana**, tell us a little about him and what happened."

Diana: "**Ryan**, please don't fight with him. I just want him to divorce me."

Ryan: "Don't worry, just tell us."

Diana (crying): "He was a good person at first, that's why I loved him. But I don't know how he changed like this. He was very temperamental, so I avoided arguing with him to avoid fights. After marriage, he started reacting intensely to small things. He would get angry and fight over trivial things. Since we traveled, every time I refused something he wanted, he would hit and insult me, then apologize after calming down. Over time, he started fighting with me for talking to my mom, dad, and **Hannah** on the phone. I don't know why."

Ryan: "I'm listening, continue."

Diana: "Every time he got angry, I found him..."

Ryan: "What?"

Diana: "**Ryan**, he hates you very much."

Ryan: "Hates me! I've never met him, we've never communicated. Why does he hate me?"

Diana cries and trembles.

Ryan (hugging her): "Okay, calm down now. We're with you. I'll look for him."

Patrick: "Why didn't you tell us while you were there, **Diana**?"

Diana cries and looks at the ground.

Patrick: "**Diana**."

Diana: "I'm sorry, Dad. I didn't listen to you and Mom. I married him even though Mom didn't approve."

Ryan: "I'll leave you two alone."

But he doesn't leave and stands at the door, watching them.

Patrick: "Look at me."

Diana: "No."

Patrick: "**Diana**, I haven't loved anyone as much as I love you. Do you think I'm happy about this because my opinion was right from the beginning?"

Diana: "I should have trusted your and Mom's opinion."

Patrick: "I know, but look, you've learned a lesson. A person won't learn unless they go through a difficult situation. The harder the situation and lesson, the stronger they learn. This is the law of life, **Diana**. You'll suffer a lot to mature. Parents want to protect their children from everything in life, so they try to surround them from all sides and intervene in everything about them. But look, how would you have learned this lesson if you hadn't gone through this experience, **Diana**? Maybe this was my mistake, and fate wanted to punish me through you. So, I've learned this lesson well."

Ryan smiles at them and leaves the room.

Patrick: "You'll pass this test, don't worry. I trust you."

Ryan looks at his ringing phone.

Ryan: "**Matthew**."

Matthew: "Brother, he doesn't need surgery. I can't believe it."

Ryan: "Really!"

Matthew: "Yes, **Ryan**, I talked to the doctor. He told me his condition doesn't require surgery."

Ryan: "That's great news, **Matthew**."

Matthew: "Yes, I'm happy now."

Ryan: "So where are you?"

Matthew: "I'm going to take my siblings out for a bit."

Ryan: "Alright, go ahead. You deserve to be happy."

Matthew: "What happened with **Diana**? Any updates?"

Ryan: "Don't worry, we'll talk about it later. Go ahead."

They end the call.

Chapter Eleven

Days pass, and **Diana's** condition slowly improves with her family's support and the psychologist she sees. **Isabella** and **William** get closer to each other and her family. **Matthew** gets closer to his siblings and tries to find a way to convince **Amelia's** family. **Ryan** searches for **Victor** (his sister's husband). One day, while **Matthew** is at work, his phone rings, and he sees it's **Amelia**.

Matthew: "How are you today?"

Amelia: "He agreed, **Matthew**."

Matthew: "Who?"

Amelia: "My dad agreed to our engagement."

Matthew (standing up): "Are you joking?"

Amelia (happily): "No, I swear he agreed. I talked to him again two days ago, and today he said he agreed."

Matthew: "I can't believe it. Finally, we'll be together."

Amelia: "Yes, nothing will separate us now. I'll go tell **Isabella**. I'll be waiting for you, my fiancé. Goodbye."

Matthew: "What?"

Amelia (laughing): "My fiancé."

Matthew: "This isn't a dream."

Amelia: "No, goodbye."

Matthew: "Goodbye, my fiancée."

Amelia goes to tell **Isabella**, knowing she's in **William's** office. She knocks on the door.

William: "Come in."

Amelia: "May I come in?"

Isabella: "Come in, **Amelia**. Are your cheeks a bit red, or am I not seeing well?"

William: "When did you come to work?"

Amelia: "He agreed, everyone."

William: "Who?"

Isabella: "What?"

Amelia: "My dad agreed to my engagement to **Matthew**."

Isabella (standing up): "I can't believe it."

William: "Congratulations to you both."

Amelia: "Can you believe it, **Isabella**? I'll be his."

Isabella hugs **Amelia** and stays silent for a moment, recalling a similar scene when she told **Amelia** that her family had approved her engagement to **Ryan**. They were both so happy, as if the scene was repeating itself.

Isabella (closing her eyes and hugging her): "Congratulations, **Amelia**. You both deserve this happiness."

William (standing up): "So, let's make this joy a double celebration. What do you think?"

Amelia and **Isabella** step back and look at each other.

Amelia: "I don't understand."

William: "What do you think, **Isabella**?"

Isabella: "What do you mean?"

William: "I mean, let's have two engagements on the same day. **Amelia** and **Matthew's** engagement, and ours. I think we've come to understand each other well now, and I've given you time to think about it."

Amelia: "Yes, that's a great idea! **Isabella** and I will be brides on the same day."

Isabella stands in shock, speechless.

Amelia: "**Isabella**, come on, agree."

William: "**Isabella**, what do you think?"

Isabella: "**William**..."

William: "Don't tell me I rushed things."

Isabella: "No, I didn't say that, but..."

William: "Alright, I'll talk to your father today, but I want to know your opinion first."

Amelia (approaching her): "Agree, **Isabella**, come on."

Isabella: "Wait, let me think for a moment."

William: "Think about what, **Isabella**? I've given you your time, I've met your family, and I've gotten closer to you. What else do you want me to do?"

Isabella: "Alright, talk to my father."

Amelia: "So, congratulations to all of us."

Amelia hugs **Isabella**, and **William** smiles.

We move to **Matthew**, who goes to **Ryan's** office. They work in the same company, as **Ryan** started there about two weeks ago.

Matthew (knocking on the door): "May I come in?"

Ryan: "Come in, **Matthew**."

Matthew: "I want to talk to you."

Ryan: "I can't handle any more bad news. Everything that's happened recently is enough, brother."

Matthew: "But it's bad news, brother."

Ryan: "What?"

Matthew: "I left **Amelia**."

Ryan: "What?!?"

Matthew: "What can I do, brother? Her father didn't approve."

Ryan: "So, you leave her?"

Matthew: "What can I do, brother?"

Ryan: "Fight for her. Try again and again."

Matthew: "I won't try. She'll find someone better than me."

Ryan: "Are you a bull, brother?"

Matthew: "What?"

Ryan: "Why did you leave her? Call her now and apologize."

Matthew: "Apologize for what?"

Matthew laughs.

Ryan: "Why are you laughing? Are you happy you left the one you love?"

Matthew: "I'm laughing at you."

Ryan: "Why?"

Matthew: "Her father agreed, brother."

Ryan: "What?"

Matthew: "Her father agreed; she will be my fiancée."

Ryan: "Did he agree, or did you leave her? Which is the truth?"

Matthew: "The truth is, she'll be with me forever."

Ryan (laughing and standing up to hug him): "So, congratulations, brother."

Ryan closes his eyes, remembering the same scene with a small difference. **Ryan** tells **Matthew** that **Isabella** will truly be his. **William** agrees with **Isabella's** father for the engagement, and he tries to have it on the same day as **Matthew** and **Amelia's** engagement. **Matthew** meets his siblings outside, and **Amelia** comes to sit with them.

Amelia: "How are you both?"

Liam and **Lara**: "Fine."

Liam: "Who is she?"

Matthew: "This is **Amelia**. She will be my fiancée."

Lara: "Really!"

Matthew: "Yes, **Lara**."

Liam: "Does that mean you'll leave us again?"

Amelia (holding **Liam's** hand): "Of course not. I'll be your big sister too."

Liam pulls his hand away from her and hugs **Matthew** out of fear, unlike **Lara**, who smiles at her. **Amelia** looks at **Matthew**.

Matthew: "He'll love you over time, don't worry."

Lara: "Will we come to your engagement?"

Matthew: "Of course, **Lara**."

Lara: "So, what will you wear?"

Amelia: "I haven't decided yet. What do you think about deciding together?"

Lara: "Of course, but I don't know if Mom will agree."

Liam (whispering to **Matthew**): "I'm scared. I don't want her with us."

Matthew: "But we agreed we'd have many friends, right?"

Liam: "But..."

Matthew: "But what? Don't you trust me?"

Liam: "I trust you."

Matthew: "Then get to know **Amelia**."

Liam: "**Lara**, let's play together."

Lara: "Wait, I'm talking to **Amelia**."

Matthew: "Okay, **Lara**, play with your brother first, but don't go far from us."

Liam: "Okay."

Liam and **Lara** go to play together for a while.

Matthew: "Don't worry, **Liam** will get used to you. He treated me like this a little at first, **Amelia**, but I'm really happy you're with them. You'll be a loving mother, **Matthew**."

Matthew: "But I'm afraid I'll become like him, like my father."

Amelia: "Of course not. You'll be a loving father."

Matthew (smiling): "And I have no doubt you'll be a loving mother. I'll talk to your father to set a date for the engagement."

Amelia: "I want to tell you something."

Matthew: "What is it?"

Amelia: "There will be two engagements, not just one."

Matthew: "How?"

Amelia: "**Isabella**."

Matthew: "What? Did **Ryan** and **Isabella** get back together? That's great news! Our joy is complete."

Amelia: "No, **Isabella** and **William**."

Matthew: "What? Are you joking?"

Amelia: "I'm not joking."

Matthew: "And they're doing it on the same day?"

Amelia: "It'll be better, believe me."

Matthew: "Better how? Do you want **Ryan** to attend **Isabella's** engagement to someone else? Or didn't you think about **Ryan** attending our engagement?"

Amelia: "I didn't think about that."

Matthew: "**Amelia**, he's my brother, and you know I won't do this to him."

Amelia: "What do you mean?"

Matthew: "I can't tell **Isabella** not to marry **William**; it's her decision. But I won't let my brother suffer like this."

Amelia: "Suffer? Isn't he the one who left her to suffer and went away? This means he won't be affected by seeing her with someone else."

Matthew: "Whose idea is this?"

Amelia: "**William** wanted us all to be happy, and I think it's a good idea."

Matthew: "Did you decide this on your own? Did **Isabella** agree to this joke?"

Amelia: "**Matthew**, listen to me. I know **Ryan** is like your brother, and **Isabella** is like my sister, but the truth is, they won't be together again."

Matthew: "Not like my brother, but he is my brother, **Amelia**. I can't believe you did this."

Amelia: "Then tell him, and you'll see that it won't matter to him."

We then switch to **Ryan's** house, where the door is being knocked on loudly.

Hannah opens the door to find **Victor**, **Diana's** husband, standing in front of her.

Victor (angrily): "Where is she?"

Hannah: "What do you want?"

Victor: "I want my wife."

Patrick comes to the sound of **Victor**.

Patrick: "Whose wife? You will divorce my daughter. Enough with what happened."

Victor (sarcastically): "Divorce her!"

Diana comes out of her room, stands, and starts trembling as she did the first time she came back.

Victor (approaching her): "Come on, we're leaving."

Ryan comes in from outside and sees him.

Ryan: "What do you want? Stay away from my sister."

Victor turns to **Ryan**.

Ryan: "**Victor**, why did you come here?"

Patrick: "Do you know each other?"

Diana hides behind her father.

Hannah: "This is **Victor**."

Ryan: "What?"

Victor: "How do you take my wife from me?"

Ryan: "Whose wife? Is that you? But why?"

Victor: "Figure it out yourself. **Diana**, come on, these people won't protect you from me."

Patrick: "Get out of here."

Ryan (grabbing **Victor** tightly): "What do you want from me? Wasn't what happened to me because of you enough? I left the country and left it because of you. Wasn't all that enough? And you married my sister and hurt her too?"

Victor: "But I didn't marry her against her will."

Patrick: "How do you know each other?"

Ryan: "This is **Victor**, he was with me in the same school and of the same age."

Diana speaks fearfully and with a trembling voice from behind her father.

Diana: "The same age? How? He's a year younger than me."

Ryan: "Did you lie about your age too? What's your problem with me?"

Victor: "Yes, I lied because I hate you."

Ryan: "I know, but why?"

Victor: "Do you want to take everything?"

Ryan: "What did I take from you?"

Victor: "I won't argue with you. **Diana**, let's go."

Ryan: "**Diana** won't come with you. You will divorce her, **Victor**, and stop this harm."

Victor: "I'll chase you forever."

Ryan: "Alright, your problem is with me. My sister hasn't done anything wrong."

Victor: "Yes, her fault is that you're her brother."

Hannah: "You're crazy. You're not a normal person."

Ryan: "**Victor**, divorce my sister. This problem is between you and me."

Victor: "I won't divorce her."

Patrick: "What do you want from us, **Victor**?"

Victor: "I won't divorce her; she's, my wife."

Ryan: "I don't want you in her life."

Victor: "It's none of your business. **Diana**, come on."

Diana: "No, I want you to leave."

Ryan: "Leave now. If you don't divorce her, there will be other consequences."

Ryan pushes **Victor** out and closes the door. **Hannah** hugs her sister.

Ryan: "Don't worry, I'll solve everything."

Eleanor: "What's the problem between you and him?"

Ryan: "I don't know, Mom. We fought once, and I don't know why he hates me so much."

Eleanor: "That's not a reason for all this hatred, **Ryan**."

Hannah: "Mom, **Diana** is trembling badly."

Ryan: "I'll call the doctor and talk to him."

After **Ryan** talks to the doctor...

Ryan: "He says she should take the sedative and sleep."

Eleanor: "How long will she stay like this?"

Ryan: "The doctor says what happened to her is normal because it causes her extreme fear. Every time she sees him; she'll be in this state until she improves."

Hannah: "But she was getting better."

Ryan: "But she saw him, so we're back to square one."

Patrick: "**Hannah**, give her the sedative, come on."

Hannah: "Okay, Dad."

Ryan's phone rings.

Ryan: "Hello."

Matthew: "I'm downstairs at your house. I need to talk to you about something important."

Ryan: "What?"

Matthew: "**Ryan**, I'm waiting for you downstairs."

Ryan hangs up and goes down to meet him.

Ryan: "What?"

Matthew: "I want to talk a little."

Ryan: "Do you remember **Victor**?"

Matthew: "**Victor**!"

Ryan: "Yes, **Victor**, who we fought with in our childhood."

Matthew: "Did he threaten you again?"

Ryan: "No, but he's **Diana's** husband."

Matthew: "Her husband, how?"

Ryan: "He wanted to continue his revenge, so he married her without my knowledge and told them he's a year younger than her."

Matthew: "But I don't understand why he hates you so much."

Ryan: "I don't know. All that matters to me now is that he leaves my sister alone."

Matthew: "Is **Diana,** okay?"

Ryan: "We went back to square one when she saw him."

Matthew: "Leave this matter to me."

Ryan: "What will you do? Wait, what's the important thing you wanted to talk to me about?"

Matthew: "Not now."

Ryan: "What happened, **Matthew**?"

Matthew: "You'll be angry."

Ryan: "Nothing matters to me anymore. Everything I feared has already happened."

Matthew: "**William** proposed to **Isabella** and she agreed. They've set the engagement date for the same day as my and **Amelia's**."

Ryan: "Okay."

Matthew: "Okay! You won't leave me, right?"

Ryan: "Leave you! What are you saying? Of course not."

Matthew: "Aren't you angry?"

Ryan: "No."

Matthew: "**Ryan**, get angry or cry, do something."

Ryan: "No, I'll go up now. Maybe they need something."

Matthew: "Are you really, okay?"

Ryan (walking away): "Goodbye."

Ryan's inner thoughts: (Did you hear the sound of my heart breaking now? Of course, you did. Is everything I feared really happening before my eyes in the most impossible way? I was sure our path was one. We separated, but we'd come back someday. But now, will I really see her beside him, wearing a wedding dress for someone else? She'll belong to someone else. I'll have no right to tell her she's beautiful today, yesterday, and tomorrow. I wish I had never returned at all. This is the greatest loss I've suffered since coming back. No, this is the greatest loss I've suffered in my entire life. Maybe it was a childish love that ended, as everyone told us before.)

Chapter Twelve

The next day, **Matthew** and **Ryan** meet at the company, specifically in **Ryan's** office, sitting across from each other.

Matthew: "The engagement is tomorrow."

Ryan: "Okay."

Matthew: "I won't agree, don't worry. If necessary, I'll postpone my engagement."

Ryan: "No, don't worry. It doesn't matter to me anymore. Of course, I'll attend my brother's engagement, and I'll also bring **Fiona**."

Matthew: "**Ryan**, nothing matters to me except you. You know that."

Ryan: "And your happiness matters to me, brother. All I'm thinking about now is **Diana**."

Matthew: "Yes, you reminded me. We'll go back to teach him a lesson."

Ryan: "That's what I thought too. So, our appointment is after your engagement."

Matthew: "No, today."

Ryan: "Do you want to attend your engagement with a face showing signs of fighting?"

Matthew: "Then our appointment is the day after tomorrow."

Ryan: "Yes."

Matthew's phone rings.

Matthew: "Tell me."

Amelia: "We'll pick you up in half an hour."

Matthew: "Why?"

Amelia: "To choose the dress and suit for tomorrow."

Matthew: "Okay, but wait, did you say 'we'?"

Amelia: "Yes, **Isabella** and **William** are with me."

Matthew: "Are you crazy, **Amelia**? I won't go with him."

Amelia: "What's wrong, **Matthew**?"

Matthew: "Then go with them, I won't come."

Amelia: "**Matthew**, I want your opinion."

Matthew: "Then we'll go alone."

Amelia: "I want **Isabella** to be with me."

Matthew: "I'm tired of this, **Amelia**."

Ryan (speaking in a low voice): "Go, don't leave her alone."

Matthew: "Okay, **Amelia**, I'll come."

They all go to buy their outfits for the next day.

Isabella: "**Amelia**, what do you think of this?"

Amelia: "It's beautiful. You look like an angel."

William: "The dress has added extra beauty when you wore it. I'm very lucky you'll be by my side."

Isabella remembers when she went with him to buy their engagement dress. He said the same sentence that **William** just said. **Amelia** stands beside her.

Amelia: "**Isabella**, are you okay?"

Isabella snaps out of her reverie.

Isabella: "Yes, I'll take this dress, but I want it in another color."

Shop assistant: "What color?"

Isabella: "Blue."

Amelia (approaching her): "That's his favorite color. Why are you wearing it now?"

Matthew: "What? Are all the other colors gone and only blue is left?"

Isabella: "Check if it's available in blue."

William: "But this color is beautiful."

Isabella: "I love blue."

Shop assistant: "Yes, we have it in blue."

Isabella: "Good, then I'll try it."

Amelia (holding her hand): "What are you doing?"

Isabella: "It's my favorite color."

Amelia: "**Isabella**, wake up from these illusions. You're with someone else now."

Isabella: "Look for a dress for yourself, come on."

Isabella tries on the blue dress, which is tight at the top, off-shoulder, and wide at the bottom. **Amelia** wears a wide burgundy dress.

Amelia: "What do you think?"

Matthew: "Isn't there another color?"

Amelia: "Why? Isn't this good?"

Matthew: "The dress is good, but I don't agree with the color."

Isabella: "I saw it in red. I think it would be better."

Matthew: "Then let's try it."

Amelia: "Where?"

Isabella: "I'll come with you."

William: "Shall we talk a bit until they come back?"

Matthew: "I need to make an important call."

William: "**Matthew**, I know you don't like me because of him, but isn't that a little unfair?"

Matthew: "Unfair? The real unfairness is proposing to a girl when you know she loves someone else."

William: "We all have our pasts, **Matthew**. I have no right to judge someone based on their past. What matters to me now is what she'll do after I enter her life."

Matthew: "Buddy, they still love each other."

William: "But it's not love."

Matthew: "Really! Then what is it?"

William: "Possessive love, maybe habit, nothing more."

Matthew: "**William**, you're a good person, and that's the problem."

William: "How?"

Matthew: "I can't see anyone beside her but him. He's my brother, of course, I'll stand by his side, but the more I get to know you, the more I find you're good."

William: "Then don't stand by anyone. He's your brother; yes, I know that. But I didn't hurt him, and I didn't cause them to separate."

Matthew: "But you're standing in their way now."

William: "**Matthew**, someone who loves doesn't leave the one they love, no matter what. They'll find a way to reach the one they love."

Matthew: "But he did it to protect her."

William: "Look, I don't know everything, and I have no right to know. But no matter the circumstances, he would have stayed by her side and protected her. He wouldn't have left her alone for five years, leaving her mind to slowly kill her."

Matthew: "He asked about her every day."

William: "He would have reached her directly."

Matthew: "At the time, he stayed away to protect her."

William: "Do you believe what you're saying?"

Matthew stays silent, and the shopping ends. They all get into **William's** car.

Amelia: "I'm hungry."

Matthew: "Then let's go eat something."

William: "I didn't expect us to spend all this time."

Isabella: "But we accomplished a lot and got everything."

Amelia: "I'm hungry."

William: "Okay, where should we go?"

Isabella: "Anywhere."

William: "Do you want to go to the same place we went before and met him?"

Matthew: "What do you mean?"

William: "**Isabella** said before that she liked that place."

Isabella: "I don't like that place anymore."

The next day arrives, and everyone attends the engagement held outside a large villa. The decorations are simple yet beautiful and elegant. The lighting mainly relies on the sun's rays as it is a daytime engagement. **William** and **Matthew** are inside the villa in one of the rooms.

William: "Let's go get **Isabella** and **Amelia**."

Matthew: "Wait a little until he comes."

William: "But he's late."

Matthew: "He'll come; I know he will."

Amelia's father arrives.

Amelia's father: "What are you waiting for?"

Matthew: "I'm waiting for my brother."

Amelia's father: "Come on, **Matthew**, everyone's waiting for you outside."

William: "Come on, **Matthew**."

Matthew: "But..."

William: "Come on."

Each enters the room where **Isabella** and **Amelia** are. **William** looks at **Isabella** and finds her standing in the blue dress, wearing a simple necklace around her neck and small earrings. Her hair is styled up in a circular shape, with two strands falling freely in front of her eyes.

William: "You look very beautiful." She smiles at him and says, "You too."

William is wearing a black suit with a tie matching her dress color. We go to **Amelia**, who is wearing a wide red dress with a long train, a short necklace, and long earrings. Her hair is also styled up in a circular shape. **Matthew** is wearing a black suit with a tie matching **Amelia's** dress color. Each holds their bride's hand and heads outside.

Everyone stands and applauds them as they walk down an aisle surrounded by flowers on both sides, with everyone behind the flowers. They walk, smiling. We focus a little on **Isabella** and **William**, finding her smiling and walking, holding **William's** hand, looking at all the guests, and inwardly hoping he isn't present.

Isabella spots **Ryan** standing at the end of the aisle, holding hands with a girl in a tight, short beige dress, her hair flowing in the wind. He's smiling at her, and **Isabella's** smile fades.

Ryan: "Are you starting the party without me?"

Matthew stands to hug him: "Why are you so late?"

Ryan: "I didn't miss anything, brother. I'm here."

Ryan: "Congratulations to you all."

He extends his hand to shake with **William**.

William: "Thank you. I didn't think you'd come."

Ryan: "This is my brother's engagement."

He ignores **Isabella** and extends his hand to shake with **Amelia**: "Congratulations, **Amelia**."

Looking at **Amelia** but meaning **Isabella**, he says: "I wish you true happiness that you didn't find before."

Fiona: "Congratulations to you all."

Gabriel arrives and stands next to **Ryan**.

Gabriel: "Why did you come? Do you want to ruin our happiness?"

Ryan: "What did I do? I'm congratulating them."

Everyone sits down. **Isabella** tries to ignore it, but she keeps looking at **Ryan**, seeing him holding **Fiona's** hand tightly.

The time comes for everyone to dance with their partners.

William: "Let's dance."

Isabella: "Alright."

Amelia and **Matthew** also dance.

Matthew: "Are we really going to be together? I still can't believe it."

Amelia: "We've worked so hard to get to this point. Wait, is **Ryan** in his right mind? What is he trying to do?"

Matthew: "I don't know, but before you ask me, I don't agree with what he's doing."

Amelia: "Did you know?"

Matthew: "Of course not. Are they looking at each other or am I not seeing clearly?"

Isabella dances with **William**, and two seconds later, **Ryan** and **Fiona** also start dancing.

Amelia (looking at **Matthew**): "Do you see what I'm seeing?"

Matthew: "He's gone mad."

Two children run toward **Matthew**.

Children: "Didn't you wait for us?"

Matthew sees them and kneels to hug them.

Matthew: "Hello, I thought you wouldn't come."

Liam: "You look very handsome today." He looks at **Amelia**: "And you too."

Amelia: "Really!"

Lara: "Yes, you're beautiful."

Matthew: "Who brought you?"

Matthew's mother arrives.

Matthew's mother: "I did."

Matthew stands up, looking at her without smiling.

Matthew: "Hello."

Amelia greets her: "Hello."

Matthew's mother: "Congratulations to you both."

She approaches **Matthew** and says: "Someone you love very much has come."

Matthew looks to see his sister, **Ruby**, approaching him.

Ruby: "Brother."

Matthew (joyfully): "Ruby."

Ruby (hugging him): "I missed you so much."

Matthew: "I didn't expect this surprise. Where are your husband and son?"

Ruby: "I told you on the phone he has work, and so do I. So, I'll leave right after your engagement."

She goes to hug **Amelia**.

Amelia (in a low voice): "Thank you."

Ruby: "He's, my brother."

Amelia: "He was sad you wouldn't be with us on a day like this."

Ruby: "And you, thank you for not leaving him alone."

Ruby steps away: "I'll go talk to **Ryan**."

We switch to **Fiona** and **Ryan**.

Fiona: "Are you trying to make her jealous?"

Ryan: "This is the first time we're dancing together."

Fiona: "**Ryan**, are you okay?"

Ryan: "I'm lucky to be with you now."

Fiona: "**Ryan**."

Ryan: "What? Wait, that's **Ruby**."

Fiona: "**Ruby** who?"

Ryan lets go of **Fiona's** hand.

Ryan: "I didn't expect you to come."

Ruby: "**Amelia** talked to me two days ago and told me to come."

Ryan: "I'm happy you came."

Ruby: "Who's this?"

Ryan: "**Fiona**."

Fiona: "This is **Ruby**, **Matthew's** sister."

Fiona: "Nice to meet you."

Ruby: "Nice to meet you too."

Ruby looks at **Ryan**: "Did you really agree to what's happening?"

Ryan doesn't answer.

Ruby: "I'll go talk to her."

Ruby talks to **Isabella**. The time comes for exchanging rings. **Matthew** takes the ring, and **Amelia** looks at him, smiling. Everyone claps. **Ruby** hugs **Matthew**, and **Ryan** hugs him, smiling. The time comes for **William** and **Isabella**. He stands in front of her and let's go of **Fiona's** hand. At that moment, he looks at the ring she's about to wear, his breathing becomes heavier, and so does hers. She puts on a fake smile until she finally wears the ring. He closes his eyes.

Matthew puts his hand on **Ryan's** shoulder, and **Fiona** holds his hand. He opens his eyes to see **William** wearing his ring. Everyone congratulates them. Suddenly, **Ryan** disappears from the crowd. **Isabella** searches for him but can't find him. She goes to **Matthew**.

Isabella: "Where did he go?"

Matthew: "Why?"

Isabella: "**Matthew**, where is he?"

Matthew: "Do you want him to see your new ring?"

Isabella: "**Matthew**..."

Matthew: "He went that way."

Isabella: "Is she with him?"

At that moment, **Fiona** arrives.

Fiona: "Where did he go?"

Isabella goes to speak with **William**.

Isabella: "I'll be back in a bit."

William: "Where to?"

Isabella: "I'll come back."

William: "Alright."

Isabella heads in the direction **Ryan** went, searching for him. She finds him sitting alone, eyes closed.

Isabella: "Are you happy now with what's happening? What do you want, **Ryan**? Why did you do all this?"

Ryan opens his eyes and says steadily: "Did you wear his ring?"

Isabella: "Yes, what's it to you?"

Ryan stands up and says: "Since when has your business not been my business, **Isabella**?"

Isabella: "Since you left me."

Ryan: "Was there no color left but blue for you to wear?"

Isabella: "Yes, it's my favorite color."

Ryan: "Really? And your hair is no longer free as it used to be!"

Isabella: "Freedom isn't in the hair."

Ryan: "Do you want to know now why I left you and went away?"

Isabella: "I don't want to know."

Ryan: "I left to protect you."

Isabella: "Have you learned to lie too?"

Ryan: "I'm not lying. Do you remember **Victor**?"

Isabella: "**Victor** who?"

Ryan: "The guy **Matthew** and I fought with along with five others, one of whom was named **Victor**."

Isabella: "I don't remember any of that. And what does that have to do with your travel?"

Ryan: "**Victor** hates me and tried to hurt me in every way. He knew I loved you, so he threatened me with you."

Isabella: "I don't believe you."

Ryan: "**Isabella**, I didn't leave willingly. I left to keep you safe."

Isabella: "Then why did you come back?"

Ryan: "I couldn't bear the exile any longer. I lost everything I built abroad and had no choice but to return."

Isabella: "That means you didn't come back for me."

Ryan: "But he hurt **Diana**."

Isabella: "What?"

Ryan: "**Diana** was married to **Victor**."

Isabella: "How?"

Ryan: "**Victor** worked at a company and recommended **Diana** to work with him. She did, and **Victor** lied to her, saying he was only a year younger than her. He never told her that we were enemies. I wanted to tell you the full truth now. At the time of my travel, I couldn't tell you because, as I said, he threatened to hurt you if I didn't leave willingly. I never loved anyone but you, and I never will."

Isabella, tears filling her eyes: "Did you remember all this now? Wait, yes, this is the perfect time to tell me all this. You want to ruin my happiness, to bring me back to you again. But that won't happen. I'll tell you one last thing: I never loved anyone like I loved you, but no one hurt me as much as you did. So go back to where you belong, because I no longer belong to you. Even after knowing the truth, I won't forgive you."

Ryan: "Ruin your happiness? Are you really happy with him? Wake up, **Isabella**, this is marriage. There's no turning back from this. You're wearing another man's ring now."

Isabella: "And you held another woman's hand, **Ryan**. You have no right to judge me after everything you did."

Ryan: "You know I'll never forget all this. There's no turning back from this. Remember, even when I left, it was to protect you. Now you're leaving me and going to another man."

Isabella: "Is that all that matters to you? That I went to someone else? But it doesn't matter that we're no longer together."

Ryan: "Do you doubt my love for you after all this? Then I can't say anything more to you. I told you the truth so it wouldn't stand between us."

Isabella: "But this barrier wasn't destroyed, even after knowing the truth."

Ryan: "Then I wish you true happiness with him. Maybe you'll find the happiness with him that you couldn't find with me."

Isabella: "And I wish you happiness with her."

Isabella walks away, tears filling her eyes, not looking back. **Ryan** sits back down alone and sighs.

Ryan's inner thoughts: (I never imagined I'd be here, seeing you beside someone else, looking at me and smiling at him.)

Fiona arrives and sits next to him.

Fiona: "Do you want to talk?"

Ryan (eyes closed): "I don't want to break your heart. You don't deserve this from me."

Fiona (smiling): "Since when?"

Ryan: "I really apologize."

Fiona: "Do you want to leave?"

Ryan: "No, I'll go back to the party."

Fiona: "How can you do this?"

Ryan: "I do it so I don't leave my brother. Wait, this is what I want to ask you: how can you do this?"

Fiona: "I don't know. Every time I want to leave, part of me tells me to stay by your side."

Ryan: "Let's go back to the party."

They return together. **Matthew** sees **Ryan** and approaches him.

Matthew: "Are you okay?"

Ryan: "Yes."

Matthew: "**Ryan**, if you want to leave, I won't be upset."

Ryan: "No, I'll stay with you."

Matthew: "**Ryan**..."

Ryan: "I won't cause any trouble, don't worry."

The day ends with everyone happy except for two. Everyone goes home after a long day. **Isabella** sits in her room in her dress, refusing to talk to anyone. She sits specifically on her bed, holding that one picture that survived the flames and wasn't burned. Or rather, she didn't want to burn it like the others.

That picture we described before, taken from their engagement party, their eyes full of joy. She looks at it and remembers that moment, then recalls what happened today and how he looked at her and what he told her.

We move to him and find him sitting in his room, feeling empty inside, lost in his memories. He can't continue amidst all this and doesn't have the right to withdraw or escape. How can he find a solution to all these problems? He hates closing his eyes because every time he does, he sees her standing in front of him, smiling. He snaps out of his reverie at the sound of his phone ringing. He looks at the phone and sees it's **Fiona** calling.

Ryan: What happened?

Fiona: I know you're not okay, so let's go out for a bit.

Ryan: I don't want to. I'll go to sleep soon. Tomorrow will be a long day for me.

Fiona: Then let's talk on the phone for a bit.

Ryan: **Fiona**, I'm really okay, but I want to be alone now.

Fiona: I don't believe you.

Ryan: I'm fine.

Fiona: But your voice doesn't say that.

Ryan: Yes, because I'm a little tired. I'll hang up now.

Fiona: Okay, as you wish.

The day ends, and the next day comes. **Matthew** and **Ryan** meet at the company. **Matthew** goes to **Ryan**'s office and knocks on the door.

Matthew: Can I come in?

Ryan: Of course, brother.

Matthew enters and sits on the chair in front of **Ryan**.

Matthew: I'm listening to you.

Ryan: I feel like I ran the whole way, stumbled, and continued just because I love walking on this path. Then someone else came and reached the end without struggling like I did.

Matthew: But...

Ryan: But what, **Matthew**? But what? I told her the truth yesterday.

Matthew: Yesterday! Did you think she would change her mind yesterday?

Ryan: I don't know. I thought she still wanted me, but no.

Matthew: Actually, **William** is a good person.

Ryan: And am I a bad person, **Matthew**?

Matthew: Of course not. What I mean is...

Ryan interrupts him, stands up, and goes to the balcony: Why, brother? Why did we reach this point? I still don't know what mistake I made to pay this price.

Matthew, still sitting: Brother, I think it's over.

Ryan, looking at him: But I still love her. Damn it, I still love her despite everything that happened.

He puts his hands over his heart and says: Here, it doesn't believe, brother, that she will be with someone else. Here, it still tells me she will be mine and that all this is nonsense. I haven't loved anyone else. I can't. I've seen countless girls, but I haven't looked at any of them the way I look at her. I try to pretend in front of her and everyone that I don't care about her, but I feel like someone ripped my heart out.

Matthew stands beside him and puts his hand on his shoulder: Brother, it will pass.

Ryan: How? How did I let this happen?

Matthew: Do you want me to talk to her?

Ryan: No.

Matthew: Should I ask **Amelia**?

Ryan: No, we'll go to **Victor**!

Matthew: How can you do this? We're talking about her, and suddenly you switch to **Victor**, and your expressions change completely.

Ryan: Because my sister needs me. I won't leave her.

Matthew: Okay, we'll go and confront him.

Ryan: No, we'll try to talk to him first.

Matthew: What! Are you scared?

Ryan: Of course not, but I promised **Diana** I wouldn't fight.

Matthew: But how will we reach him?

Ryan: I got his phone number from **Diana**, talked to him before coming to work, and arranged to meet him shortly.

Matthew: Brother, I'm afraid he'll bring men with him.

Ryan: Did you forget who **Victor** is?

Matthew: Because I didn't forget, I said that. I know he's a coward, so he'll bring men with him.

Ryan: No, he won't.

Matthew: **Ryan**, don't be delusional.

Ryan: I'm not delusional. Let's go.

Matthew: But the work isn't finished!

Ryan: I know. I got permission for both of us from the manager today.

Matthew, surprised: Did he agree?

Ryan pushes him towards the door and says: Come on, brother, let's go.

They go to the agreed place, and **Ryan** stops the car.

Matthew: Is this the place?

Ryan: Yes.

Matthew: **Ryan**...

Ryan: Don't worry.

Matthew: How? There's no one here but us.

Ryan: I know, but don't worry. Let's get out because he's here.

Matthew: Okay.

They get out of the car, and **Victor** gets out of his car.

Ryan: I expected you wouldn't come alone.

Victor laughs and stays silent.

Matthew: Did something hit your head, **Victor**, to make **Diana** pay the price? Wasn't it enough that you left **Isabella** and disappeared for five years!

Victor: But I came back.

Ryan: **Victor**, this problem is between us. **Diana** has nothing to do with it.

Victor: How? She's your sister.

Ryan: **Victor**, look, I'm trying hard to control my anger.

Victor: Why?

Ryan: How did you marry my sister without my knowledge? And you lied to her too, raised your hand against her several times, causing her psychological and physical harm. Do you think I'll forgive you for all this? Why do you hate me? Okay, you hate me, but what did **Diana** and **Isabella** do to deserve this?

Victor: How did you know?

Matthew: Know what!

Victor: That it's **Isabella**'s turn now.

Ryan: What? **Victor**, believe me, I won't leave you. **Isabella** and **Diana**, no, **Victor**.

Victor: Don't worry, she won't suffer like **Diana**.

Ryan approaches him to hit him, but **Matthew** holds him back.

Matthew: **Ryan**, calm down.

Matthew: **Victor**, what's your problem?

Victor: There's no problem.

Ryan: Look, I'm right here. Do you want to get rid of me? Fine, I agree, but don't hurt my sisters and **Isabella**.

Victor laughs and says: What? Did **Isabella**'s engagement make you this calm?

Matthew approaches him: **Ryan**, please calm down. He's not alone.

Ryan, loudly: Is **William** with you?

Victor laughs and stays silent.

Matthew: What's with the coldness? Are you mentally ill, boy?

Victor: Yes, just like you, **Matthew**.

Ryan: Will you make him stay away from her, or should I do it my way?

Victor: But you couldn't make him stay away from her. Did you forget their engagement was yesterday?

Ryan: Believe me, I know exactly how to make him stay away from her and how to make you regret everything you've done and are doing.

Victor: You're going to make me angry now, and I came to tell you some good news.

Ryan: What!

Victor: I'm going to divorce **Diana**. I don't want her anymore, and I'll stay away from her.

Ryan: And she doesn't want you. You'll divorce her today.

Victor: Okay, but I'm not finished talking.

Ryan: You'll stay away from her too and make him leave her life.

Victor: You're the one who will choose this.

Ryan: Choose what? Are you sick?

Victor: You said yes before. You said it to your brother five minutes ago. **Diana** or **Isabella**.

Ryan: What?

Matthew: You've gone too far, **Victor**. Enough.

Victor: I think I presented a very difficult choice. If I were you, I would choose my sister, of course. But of course, my beloved is also difficult. But wait, she's not your beloved anymore.

Ryan gets angry and hits him.

Matthew: No, no, wait, **Ryan**.

Victor falls to the ground, and **Ryan** continues to hit him.

Ryan says angrily: What do you want from me? Why do you hate me so much? I left her because of you and left the country. You promised me you wouldn't hurt her when I stayed away from her, and when I came back, I found you married to my sister.

Matthew: **Ryan**, leave him. Enough.

Victor laughs while being hit, and the place fills with men.

Matthew: Brother, I think we're going to get beaten now.

Ryan moves away from **Victor** and stands with **Matthew**. **Victor** sits with signs of the beating on his face.

Victor says to his men: Let them go.

Matthew: Come on, **Ryan**, let's go.

Matthew: I'll drive the car until you calm down.

They get in the car.

Ryan: We'll go to her.

Matthew: I know.

They go to her workplace, specifically to **William**'s office, and open the door without knocking. A girl follows them and talks to **Ryan**.

The girl says to him: But Dr. **William** has a meeting now.

William: What's this?

The girl: I tried to stop them, but...

Ryan interrupts her and says loudly: Look, you'll leave now and leave **Isabella** and go out of her life completely. If I find you trying to get close to her again, you'll find someone else in front of me.

The girl to **William**: Should I call security?

William stands up and says calmly: No, there's no problem. Go. Then he looks at the people sitting.

William says to them: We'll continue the meeting later.

Everyone leaves the room, and **Ryan** and **Matthew** remain.

Matthew: I thought you were a good person.

William, putting his hand on the ring he's wearing: Sit down. Do you think your behavior is right? This is my workplace, not a place for fighting.

Ryan: You'll leave **Isabella** now.

Isabella and **Amelia** arrive.

Isabella: Leave who? Are you asking him to leave me like you did?

Matthew: How did you know we were here?

Amelia: From his voice.

Ryan: Look, you'll leave her.

Isabella: Are you crazy?

Ryan: Look, **Isabella**, he's not a good person as you think. He will hurt you. **Victor** is behind him.

William: What? I don't know anyone named **Victor**.

Ryan: I've overlooked a lot since you came back, but this is enough. She's my fiancée now. How will I hurt her?

Ryan: Yes, but I won't let you hurt her, so you'll leave her.

Isabella: Did you think I didn't believe your story about traveling and leaving me, so you came now to tell another story?

Amelia: What? Why did he leave you?

Ryan approaches her: **Isabella**, I didn't lie to you. Believe me, everything I'm saying is true.

William: **Ryan**, I think you forgot that her fiancé is standing in front of you. Stay away from her and leave here. Enough.

Ryan: What's the price you'll take? I'll give you double, but leave her.

William: Price for what? And who is **Victor**? Why would I hurt her? I've endured all this for her only, but you're going too far.

Matthew: **Victor** told us the truth.

William: What truth? Come on, **Matthew**, please take your friend and leave here.

Ryan: I won't let you hurt her.

William: **Ryan**, wake up from this dream. She's my fiancée now.

Ryan: I know.

William: So what?

Isabella interrupts and stands between them.

Isabella: Enough, **Ryan**. This is my decision.

Ryan: Do you really believe him and not me?

Isabella: Leave here, **Ryan**. If he wanted to hurt me, he would have done it before.

Matthew: **Isabella**...

Isabella: Leave here.

Matthew takes **Ryan**, and they go outside. **Amelia** follows them.

Amelia: **Matthew**...

They both stop.

Ryan: **Amelia**, don't leave her.

Amelia, ignoring **Ryan**: **Matthew**, what's happening? Who's **Victor**?

Matthew: Didn't she tell you?

Amelia: Tell me what?

Matthew: She'll tell you, but **Ryan** is telling the truth.

Amelia: But **William** really loves her, so how would he hurt her?

Matthew: It turns out he was lying.

Ryan: I'll leave you both alone. I'll wait for you in the car.

Ryan takes a step away from them, then stops and looks back at **Amelia**.

Ryan: Please, **Amelia**, don't let her get hurt.

He leaves them and we return to **William** and **Isabella** who are still standing in the room.

William: What will happen, **Isabella**? Are you going to continue this way?

Isabella, sitting in front of him: Is what he said true?

William: Are you joking?

Isabella: No, but I...

William: You still believe him. Will he always be between us?

Isabella: He's not between us.

William goes to sit on the chair in front of her.

William: What more can I do? Do you think I didn't notice how you looked at him a while ago, **Isabella**?

Isabella: No, no...

William closes his eyes: Look, **Isabella**, I'll respect your decision.

Isabella: Will you leave me like he wants?

William opens his eyes, stands up, and says angrily: Not like he wants, **Isabella**. I'm doing this like you want. You look at me with fear now because of what he said.

Isabella: I didn't believe him.

William: **Isabella**, I won't allow this. I won't allow you to be with me but your heart is with him.

Isabella: Of course not.

William: Then decide what you're going to do.

Isabella: If I wanted him, I would have gone with him, **William**.

William: Okay, **Isabella**.

Their discussion ends there, and **Isabella** goes to **Amelia**'s room to wait for her to talk. **Amelia** opens the door and finds her sitting, waiting.

Isabella: Where were you?

Amelia: I was talking with **Matthew**.

Isabella: Did he say anything to you?

Amelia: No, he said you would tell me.

Isabella: Then sit down, I want to talk with you.

Amelia: What happened?

Isabella tells her what **Ryan** said to her yesterday.

Isabella: That's everything, and you know what happened today. **William** wanted me to decide what to do because he saw how I looked at him.

Amelia: He's right, **Isabella**.

Isabella: What do I do now? Whom should I believe?

Amelia: I don't know, but **Matthew** told me **Ryan** is telling the truth, but I don't think **William** would hurt you.

Isabella: Then what do I do?

Amelia: I don't really know, what do you feel?

Isabella: I feel that he loves me and won't hurt me.

Amelia: **Isabella**, take some time to think.

Isabella: He told me he left me to protect me. How come you never told me that before?

Amelia: Because I didn't know.

Isabella: How? Didn't **Matthew** tell you?

Amelia: No, he didn't tell me anything back then or even after.

There's a knock-on **Amelia**'s door.

Amelia: Come in.

William: I expected you'd be here.

Isabella: **William**, what happened?

William, standing in front of her: Nothing, I wanted to apologize for getting angry with you.

Isabella: But you're right.

William: But I got a little angry.

He approaches her and looks at **Amelia**.

Amelia: I'll leave you two alone then.

Amelia leaves.

William: Look, **Isabella**, I love you. I won't hurt you. How does someone who loves hurt the one they love?

Isabella: Then why did he say that?

William: Are you asking why? Because he doesn't want us to be together, **Isabella**. I've tried so much with you, and when he came back, I felt like we went back to square one. You look at me as if I'm a stranger, and you look at him as if he's everything to you. I don't know why you agreed to our engagement, but I'll always love you.

Isabella: But I...

William: Wait, **Isabella**. I always told myself I wouldn't love another girl after her, but when I saw you the first time, I felt everything was okay.

Isabella: You told me that before. I'm sorry if I caused you distress, but I didn't mean to.

William: Please, **Isabella**, think about it again.

Isabella: But I'm afraid, **William**.

William: Of me?

Isabella: **William**...

William: Do you remember the day we talked honestly about you and me?

Isabella: The day I told you about her and you told me about him?

William: Yes, you can talk to me like that again, as if we're friends.

Isabella: **William**, what's between me and him is more than just two people with a love story that ended. It won't end in just a day or two. It will always be there because of **Amelia** and **Matthew**.

William: I know. He doesn't matter to me, nor do his feelings for you. What matters to me are your feelings for him, **Isabella**.

William: I feel he's always between us like a barrier. You didn't look at me the way you looked at him. **Isabella**, do you still love him?

Isabella: No, I don't know.

William: You don't know!

Isabella: Look, I really found myself with you. I felt I came back to life again.

William: I know. I see you different from the first day you came here, but you still love him. Maybe you love me as a brother or a friend, but not like him.

Isabella: **William**, you're repeating what he did. You're leaving me without a logical reason.

William: Without a logical reason! I'll bear everything in life except being with you while you look at him like that because it's called betrayal.

Isabella: Betrayal!

William: Yes, betrayal, **Isabella**.

Isabella: I apologize; it won't happen again. I promise. But you won't hurt me, right?

William: Are you still really asking?

Isabella: Yes, I just want to be reassured. Is that too much to ask?

William: I promise, but you'll think about this topic again.

Isabella: Okay.

Their conversation ends there. The day ends after a lot of work, and **Isabella** returns home. She sees a message from **Ryan** sent from **Matthew**'s phone that she missed due to her busy day. She reads it in her room.

(Message: Please don't believe him. You might think I'm doing this out of jealousy, but the truth is he will hurt you. I will protect you from him with or without your approval. I won't leave you to this stubbornness. Think carefully about everything.)

She sees the message and calls him.

Ryan: **Isabella**.

Isabella: I called to tell you something. Please, stop, **Ryan**. Stop everything. Let me do what I want in my life.

Ryan: I'll leave you, but at least I won't let you get hurt.

Isabella: You're the person who hurts me the most, **Ryan**.

Ryan: No, I didn't mean...

Isabella: If you have any love for me, leave me alone. Don't interfere in anything related to me.

Ryan: What? Do you really want to continue with him?

Isabella: Yes, I want him. I want to hang up now.

Ryan: I still love you, **Isabella**, and always will.

They end the call, and **Ryan** looks at his phone and finds a message from **Victor**.

(Message: Have you decided?)

Ryan replies: (I've decided. You won't hurt either of them.)

Victor: (But that's a third option that doesn't exist.)

Chapter Thirteen

Ryan: Please, **Victor**, I'll do anything you want, but **Isabella** and **Diana** have no fault.

Victor: That means you'll leave the decision to me.

Ryan: Why do you hate me so much?

Victor doesn't reply. There's a knock-on **Ryan**'s door.

Ryan: Come in.

Hannah: **Ryan**, there's a guest outside who wants to see you.

Ryan: A guest?

Hannah: Yes.

Ryan goes out and finds **Fiona** sitting with his mother, talking.

Eleanor looks at **Ryan**.

Ryan, looking at **Fiona**: **Fiona**, what are you doing here? And how did you find my house?

Eleanor: What are you saying, my son? Did I teach you to treat guests like this?

Fiona: Did you forget I came here before when **Diana** returned?

Ryan: Yes, I remember. Why did you come?

Eleanor: **Ryan**.

Ryan: Mom, can we talk for a bit?

Hannah: Did you forget the rules, brother, or what?

Ryan: Then let's talk outside, **Fiona**.

Fiona stands: We'll meet again, aunt. I liked you a lot.

Eleanor: Me too.

Fiona, moving: Goodbye, **Hannah**.

Hannah: Goodbye.

Ryan: Come on, **Fiona**. I'm angry.

Fiona: Wait, I want to meet your father and **Diana**.

Ryan: **Fiona**.

Fiona: Next time then.

They go outside.

Eleanor to **Hannah**: Did you see? I think she suits him very well.

Hannah: What are you thinking, mom?

Eleanor: Will he remain single like this? Of course not.

They go outside to talk.

Ryan: Why did you come?

Fiona: I wanted to see you. I thought you wanted to talk, so I came... **Ryan**, why are you treating me like this?

Ryan: Because I don't want to hurt you.

Fiona: But you don't hurt me.

Ryan: **Fiona**, I'm sorry. I can't reciprocate the same feelings. It's better if you leave the country.

Fiona: Did you forget this is my country too?

Ryan: I didn't forget, but you told me before that you would never settle here. When I came back, you left everything there and came.

Fiona: What did I do wrong, **Ryan**? I came to help you, to listen to you. I know you still love her.

Ryan: Because it hurts you when I talk about her in front of you.

Fiona: I didn't tell you that.

Ryan: But I feel it. Look, from the first day we met, you've been by my side. You never hurt me even once. So why would I cause you pain like this?

Fiona: **Ryan**, please don't talk like that.

Ryan: It's my fault. I should have stopped you from the beginning.

Fiona: At least let me stay by your side for now.

Ryan: **Fiona**, please.

Fiona: If I leave, will you go back to her?

Ryan: No, wait, what do you mean?

Fiona: All I mean is that we'll remain friends, just as we always were. Talk to me about what's inside you.

Ryan: **William** will hurt her, **Fiona**. **Isabella** thinks I'm lying to make her leave him.

Fiona: **William**! How? I saw how he looks at her. I don't think so.

Ryan: Do you remember **Victor**?

Fiona: The one you told me about before and caused all this?

Ryan: Yes, him.

Fiona: Yes, I remember. What did he do?

Ryan tells her what happened.

Fiona: But I don't believe that **William** would do this.

Ryan, angrily: Why do you all trust him like that?

Fiona: Look, **Ryan**, I always believe that hidden feelings, whether love, hate, or anger, show through our eyes or perhaps our actions. Every time I looked at him, I found love inside him.

Ryan: And what do you see when you look at me?

Fiona: Anger.

Ryan: Anger!!!

Fiona: Yes, **Ryan**, anger towards everyone—**Victor**, your family, **William**, and even **Isabella**.

Ryan: Even **Isabella**? Do you believe what you're saying?

Fiona: Yes, because you thought that just by coming back, she would come back to you again. When she didn't, you got angry at her. You also feel that you did all this for her, but she did nothing for you.

Ryan, closing his eyes: I want everything to go back to the way it was.

Fiona: It won't, because it's the past, and the past doesn't come back.

Ryan, opening his eyes: Then what do I do?

Fiona: You won't hurt either of them.

Ryan: How?

Fiona: You'll leave her.

Ryan: Leave **Isabella**? Absolutely not, I will protect her too.

Fiona: That's her problem, but **Diana**...

Ryan: But he wants...

Fiona, interrupting him: He knows you love her, so he does all this.

Ryan: Okay, but what if he really hurts her and **William** is with him?

Fiona: Talk to **William** and tell him to protect her.

Ryan: And me?

Fiona: You'll protect **Diana**.

Ryan: And **Isabella** too.

Fiona: I'm tired of this. Do what you want.

Ryan: **Fiona**, why are you acting like this?

Fiona: And why are you still protecting her?

Ryan stays silent and closes his eyes.

Fiona: I'll go then.

Ryan opens his eyes and looks at her.

Ryan: Wait.

Fiona: What?

Ryan: Will you marry me?

Fiona, astonished: What? You wanted me to leave just a moment ago and told me we should stay friends, and now you want to marry me? Is this the solution you found?

Ryan: Yes, no, I don't really know, but she won't come back.

Fiona: Will you do like her and marry someone else just to make her angry?

Ryan: To stay away from her.

Fiona: Do you believe what you're saying?

Ryan: Yes, since I came back, I was thinking about how to get her back. I told her why I left, but she didn't believe me. Even now, she doesn't believe me and believes him instead.

Fiona: **Ryan**, I'll go, and we'll sit later and think. This is not a logical solution.

Ryan: And was everything that happened logical?

Fiona: I won't tell you things you already know.

Ryan: Yes, I left her, but why? To protect her. I didn't leave her because I found someone else, but she will marry him. She told me to let her do what she wants. Fine, I'll leave her.

Fiona: Fine, **Ryan**, I won't argue with you now. I'll go, and you think alone.

Ryan goes up to his house and opens the door to find his mother waiting.

Eleanor: What happened? Where did **Fiona** go?

Ryan: **Fiona** and I are just friends.

Eleanor: But she's a nice girl.

Ryan: I'll go to my room.

Ryan goes to his room and falls asleep. The next day, he goes to work, thinking about what to do when his phone rings, and he sees it's his mother.

Ryan: Mom.

Eleanor: **Victor**.

Ryan, standing up: What did he do?

Eleanor: He sent **Diana**'s divorce papers.

Ryan, sitting down happily: Really!

Eleanor: Yes.

Ryan: And **Diana**! Is she okay now?

Eleanor: Yes, but she went to her psychologist.

Ryan: Does she know?

Eleanor: Yes.

Ryan, sighing: Okay, Mom, I'll hang up now.

Matthew knocks on the door.

Ryan: **Matthew**.

Matthew, sitting in front of him: What happened? You seem happy.

Ryan: **Victor** sent the divorce papers.

Matthew: What? Really?

Ryan: Yes.

Matthew: Then everything is on the right track now.

Ryan: Yes.

Then he falls silent and remembers **Victor**'s words.

Matthew: What happened? What are you thinking about?

Ryan: I'm scared.

Matthew: Of him?

Ryan: Yes, what if he hurts her?

Matthew: **Diana**?

Ryan: **Isabella**.

Matthew: I don't think so.

Ryan: **Victor** won't back down, **Matthew**. That's why I'm worried. I need to make sure **William** really has nothing to do with **Victor**.

Matthew: **Ryan**.

Ryan: What? Okay, we won't be together again, but I won't let her get hurt because of me.

Matthew: What did you say?

Ryan: I thought about it well yesterday.

Matthew: And what did you decide?

Ryan: I decided to let go of all the ropes, but I won't let anyone hurt her no matter what. She will always be inside me.

Matthew: And **Fiona**!

Ryan: You reminded me of her. I'll call her to tell her this happy news.

Matthew: You reminded me of her!

Ryan: Go to your work, and I'll talk to **Fiona** and tell her to meet after work.

Matthew, standing up: I see you're kicking me out.

Ryan, smiling: I felt that too.

Matthew: Okay, I'll go.

Days pass, and **Diana**'s condition improves after the divorce. She returns to her life and decides to go back to work but in a different place. **Isabella** and **William** get closer to each other, and she feels reassured that **Ryan**'s words were just a lie. **Ryan** stays with **Fiona** but keeps watching **Isabella** from afar to protect her. Then, an unexpected event happens to **Ryan**. He sits in his office working when **Matthew** enters.

Matthew: **Ryan**.

Ryan, focused on his work and not looking at **Matthew**: What happened, **Matthew**?

Matthew: **Victor**.

Ryan: What happened again?

Matthew: He was arrested.

Ryan, standing up and looking at him: What? Are you joking?

Matthew, sadly: Him and my father.

Ryan: How and why?

Matthew, sitting down: I'll tell you everything, but first, I apologize.

Ryan: Why? **Matthew**, tell me.

Matthew: It turns out that **Victor** is my father's friend's son.

Ryan: And...

Matthew: My father is involved in illegal activities.

Ryan: Yes.

Matthew: Did you know?

Ryan: Yes.

Matthew: Why didn't you tell me before?

Ryan: What's **Victor**'s connection to your father?

Matthew: Why didn't you tell me, **Ryan**?

Ryan: Why should I? To break you more?

Matthew: But it's my right.

Ryan: How did you find out? And what's **Victor**'s connection to all this?

Matthew: **Victor** is his friend's son and works with him, so they were both arrested.

Ryan: How did you find out?

Matthew: From his friend.

Ryan: What?

Matthew: Since when did you know?

Ryan: Since then. You remember that **Amelia**'s father and your father were friends.

Matthew: Yes, does **Amelia** know too?

Ryan: Her father told her, and she told me. We decided not to tell you to avoid breaking you. How did you find out? I don't understand.

Matthew: Why didn't you tell me?

Ryan: I told you to avoid breaking you.

Matthew: But he's, my father.

Ryan: What?

Matthew: He made his friend call me and tell me everything, saying he wants me by his side.

Ryan: By his side in what? Are you crazy?

Matthew: He's, my father.

Ryan: Will you really help him?

Matthew, sitting and putting his hands on his head: I don't know, but I have a strange feeling I've never felt before. Maybe regret, so he did all this.

Ryan, putting his hand on **Matthew**'s shoulder: Do you want him to exploit you?

Matthew, looking at him: What?

Ryan: **Matthew**, your father thinks only of himself. He did this so you'd stand by him and help him get out.

Matthew: Am I a lawyer and I don't know it?

Ryan: No, but he knows you'll do anything for him.

Matthew: Will I leave him alone as he did with me?

Ryan: You're not alone. I'm with you, and so is **Amelia**.

Matthew: **Ryan**, I really apologize.

Ryan: Why?

Matthew: Because my father knew all this and caused all this.

Ryan: Why would your father hurt me?

Matthew: Because you're with me.

Ryan: I don't believe this, and even if it's true, it doesn't matter. I'm with you.

Matthew: But this caused you to lose **Isabella**.

Ryan: **Isabella**, but wait, **Victor** has hated me since our childhood. How?

Matthew: Yes, **Victor** hates you and wanted to hurt you, but the idea of you leaving the country and marrying **Diana** was my father's idea.

Matthew stands up and says: Try with **Isabella** again.

Ryan: Do you really think so?

Matthew: Yes, go ahead.

They go to **Isabella** and **Amelia**'s workplace, and **Ryan** enters **Isabella**'s room without knocking.

Ryan: **Isabella**.

He finds **William** and **Isabella** sitting together, and **Amelia** in front of them.

Amelia, standing up: **Matthew**, **William** and **Isabella** have set their wedding date for next week.

Ryan: What?

Matthew: **Amelia**, are you joking?

Isabella, standing in front of **Ryan**: No, she's not joking.

Matthew: But **Isabella**, look...

Ryan: Congratulations to both of you. Come on, **Matthew**.

Matthew, looking at him: What?? Wait.

Ryan: Come on, **Matthew**.

Amelia: Wait, why did you come?

Ryan: Nothing.

William: Why are you leaving? Wait, let's celebrate together.

Ryan looks into her eyes, as if he remembered everything that happened between them before he left her. He closes his eyes and goes to stand outside the lab.

Matthew: How does this lab work?

William: I don't understand what you mean.

Matthew: Every time I come; I see you all sitting here talking.

He looks at **Amelia** and says: Look, you'll leave this lab.

Isabella: **Matthew**, go after him.

Matthew: It turns out you're really naive.

Amelia: **Matthew**.

Isabella: Really!

Matthew: Yes, you don't deserve him.

Isabella: Fine.

William: Come on, **Matthew**.

Matthew goes and finds **Ryan** standing outside the lab.

Matthew: Are you okay?

Ryan: Extremely.

Matthew: What, are you joking with me?

Ryan: This time, everything is really over. I don't want her.

Matthew: But...

Ryan: But what? She will marry him? What should I wait for? Should I wait until she has children with him? I tried everything with her, but she didn't give me a second chance, **Matthew**. She didn't give me a chance.

Matthew: And you...

Ryan: What did I do? What did I do? I paid for sins I didn't commit. Will I spend the rest of my life protecting my loved ones, and what about me? Who will protect me? Fine, I'll tell you. No one, no one really. Maybe it was a naive childhood love, **Matthew**, so I won't care about her anymore. Even if he hurts her, I won't move a single step. It's all over.

Matthew hugs him.

Ryan: I'm really tired of everything. Why do I have to pay this price, and for how long?

Matthew: Everything will be fine, brother.

We return to the lab. **William**'s phone rings.

William: This is an important call. I'll take it and come back, **Isabella** and **Amelia**, okay?

Amelia looks at **Isabella** after **William** leaves.

Isabella: (Not all mistakes can be forgiven, forgotten, or overlooked. Yes, I learned the reason for his departure was to protect me, but when did I find out? After he left my heart to be consumed by doubts and confusion, left the fire inside me to grow. When I tried to extinguish it and start anew, he came back again to reignite it. The truth after it's too late is useless. Maybe we would have stayed together if he had told me the truth at the time. Maybe I would have forgiven him, but he made the decision alone and left me. He left others to mend the wounds he caused, so my heart won't forgive what happened.)

Amelia: Are you really going to marry **William**?

Isabella: We'll see what happens. Maybe yes, maybe no.

We go to **William**.

William, answering the phone: Yes, I'm going to marry her. What? No, that will never happen. It won't happen. Yes, that's my final decision.

The End